Varna halted in the trail, sniffing the air. I sniffed myself, but my smog-dulled sense of olfaction brought me no information. "What is it?" I whispered.

The answer to my question leaped into the path before us. It was the most terrifying apparition I have ever seen in my short life.

The beast was six feet long and four feet high at its powerful shoulders. A stump of tail lashed the air behind it and huge claws were unsheathed on each of the massive forepaws. It was the head that was most incredible, however. From the bared upper jaw descended two enormous scythe-like fangs, each at least a foot long.

I had stood as a child in Rancho La Brea Park and gazed in fascination at the life-like statues there, and I recognized the living engine of destruction that now crouched before me.

It was a sabre-toothed tiger.

A SPECIAL ANNOUNCEMENT TO ALL
ERB ENTHUSIASTS

Because of the widespread, continuing interest in the books of Edgar Rice Burroughs, we are listing below the names and addresses of various ERB fan club magazines. Additional information may be obtained from the editors of the magazines themselves.

—THE EDITORS

ERB-DOM MAGAZINE
Route 2, Box 119
Clinton, LA 70722

THE BURROUGHS BIBLIOPHILES
6657 Locust Street
Kansas City, Missouri 64131

ERBANIA MAGAZINE
8001 Fernview Lane
Tampa, Florida 33615

MAHARS
OF PELLUCIDAR

by
JOHN ERIC HOLMES

ace books
A Division of Charter Communications Inc.
1120 Avenue of the Americas
New York, N.Y. 10036

I

BENEATH THE EARTH'S CRUST

It is strange that I got involved in the matter transmitter project at all. The matter transmitter was invented by two physicists, Moritz and Kingsly. It had been used by them to obtain specimens of minerals from the oceans' depths or from the bottom of drill shafts. The original plan had been to use it to send rock specimens back from the bottom of the Mohole, that ill-fated project to drill through the earth's crust. When the Mohole project was abandoned due to lack of government funds, Dr. Moritz and Dr. Kingsly began investigating other uses for the device, and very surprising uses they turned out to be.

All this took place back in 1970. I was then working as a graduate student in Dr. Holmes' brain research laboratory. My background is entirely in biology. I had completed the first two years of medical school and was spending a year investigating the relationship between certain electroencephalographic brain wave patterns and intelligence. In cats. Did you ever consider designing an IQ test for cats? Think about it, it isn't easy.

As a matter of fact, I never did figure out a good way to measure intelligence in the cat. As I was getting pretty bored with the attempt, I welcomed the interruption of being called into my boss' office to discuss the idea of a new project. Dr. Holmes introduced me to Dr. Moritz who was a little guy with a dark beard and thick-lensed spectacles. I recognized his name, which pleased him, for I had read about his invention in *Scientific American.*

"What I am interested in, now that the program to penetrate the earth's crust has been abandoned by the short-sighted politicians, is other applications of the disintegrator-reintegrator principle. Kingsly and I have invested everything we had in a commercial venture utilizing our device. I'm sure it must have many practical as well as scientific applications."

Dr. Holmes interrupted, "Dr. Moritz wants to try his matter transmitter on living organisms. I assured him that living cells were too complex to be reduced to a coded series of impulses in a coaxial cable. So, he told me that they have already done it."

"Really?" I cried, looking at the two of them in disbelief. "Really, have you sent a live animal through a wire?"

"Well, not quite," said the little scientist. "What I mean is," he continued, "the subject sample is not itself transmitted through the cable. The specimen is disintegrated completely. The energy released is used to generate the signals and power the reintegrator at the receiving end." He got up and went to the blackboard at the end of the room. As he talked, he illustrated his remarks with a series of vague geometric shapes and arrows. I've seen my professors of chemistry and psychiatry use the same hieroglyphics. They aren't intended to represent real things but concepts and ideas. "The object to be transmitted is torn down by the disintegrator beam, atom by atom. The position of each atom is recorded and transmitted to the reintegrator unit over the connecting wires." He drew a line between two rectangles, one labeled DIS and the other RE. "Precise replication of molecular patterns can be

6

achieved, but we are concerned about subtle changes in the brain."

"How long does it take to transmit something?" I asked.

"Depends on the size of the object," the physicist replied, "anything over 100 grams takes several milliseconds."

"Is that all!" I exclaimed, "Only a few thousandths of a second? I was concerned about the time factor on the brain of a large animal."

"Oh," he answered confidently, "we could transmit any large animal in less than ten seconds." Little did he suspect then how important all this was to be to me later, for a "large animal" could easily be a man!

We discussed methods of studying experimental animals who had been "sent down the wire" in Moritz's laboratory. I agreed to drive out to Santa Monica the next day to collect animal specimens and, incidentally, to view the apparatus.

The Santa Monica lab turned out to be part of a large factory complex close to the ocean. Moritz and Kingsly had convinced the company directorate to finance their matter transmitter. I suppose its subsequent commercial exploitation more than justified the investment, but it must have been prodigious. The research building alone was a block long and eight stories high. Much of this space, however, was for the small atomic reactor which had powered the first experiments.

In the main lab I was introduced to Dr. Kingsly, a large blond man in his early thirties. His was the mathematical mind that had worked out the molecular-atomic pulse code without which an object put into one end of the matter transmitter would come come out the other end only a formless blob. Kingsly took my hand in a powerful grasp. "Glad to see you, Dr. West," he boomed. "I understand you're our expert on animal intelligence."

"Call me Chris," I requested, "that doctor's degree is several years away yet. And I'm not so sure about 'expert.'"

"Modesty, modesty," said the big man, putting an arm around my shoulders. I stood a good six-six, but he loomed over me. "You must call me Tiny, and our colleague here," indicating Dr. Moritz, "has been known for years simply as Doc. But come along and see our gadget."

The experimental transmitter looked rather like a conventional X-ray table except that it was enclosed in a glass box. The adjustable tabletop was 6 feet by 2 feet in size and the funnel-nosed projector loomed above it on gymbals. From the housing of the disintegrator projector a single cable led across the floor to a similar chamber at the other end of the laboratory room.

"This baby," said "Tiny", slapping the side of the enclosed chamber, "is our first model, and the one we use for biological specimens." He led me to a window overlooking a paved inner courtyard. "Out there," he pointed to what looked to me rather like an oil drilling rig with its nose stuck through a gaping hole in the cement, "is the earth borer we used to get geological samples from the crust for the Mohole project before it got scuttled. That's a better designed instrument—miniaturized, you know—with a television camera built into the disintegrator unit so you can see what you're sampling. We've cored down fifty miles with that baby and got it back up."

"Fifty miles!" I exclaimed, "How on earth could you run fifty miles of cables down into the center of the earth without snapping it?"

"Didn't have to," he replied proudly, "you can

send the full complex of information back by laser beam if you have a straight hole."

"Do the city fathers of Santa Monica know," I asked, "that you have been boring holes through the earth's crust?"

"Certainly not," he said. "Can you imagine what an earthquake scare that would set off?" He smiled, "It's all perfectly safe, of course, the hole isn't eight inches in diameter. Come see our menagerie." He gestured toward the end of the room. "I guess Doc told you we'd done some mice and a rabbit. The first mice came through dead. I've adjusted the transmitter and now they all are living at the other end. We wonder, though, if some minute change might not affect their nervous system."

"I'd like to take some back to the lab with me, but I'm really set up to study cats."

"Oh, yes, Doc told me. We went down to the pound today and got two cats for you. If you want to help me, we'll transmit one now so you can see how it's done." As an afterthought he added, "I saved the first mice, the ones that died, they're in the freezer in the next room."

"Good," I said, "I'll have to autopsy them."

We got a large friendly tomcat out of his cage and anesthetized him for the experiment. "I've never tried it without anesthesia," said Kingsly, as we gave the purring animal his injection. "I have no way of knowing, but I assume it hurts to be disintegrated."

He took the sleeping cat from my arms and went inside the transparent enclosure around the transmitter. He arranged the animal on the tabletop, adjusted the snout of the disintegrator over it and stepped out. The animal's chest rose slowly with each respiration, otherwise it was motionless.

Kingsly went to a control panel against the wall

and began adjusting a series of knobs and switches. "Ready to go!" he announced, after about five minutes of testing. "Watch the cat."

I stared at the unconscious animal. The scientist pressed a button. There was an instantaneous flash of light. The cat was gone. The table top where it had lain was bare and untouched.

"Down to the receiver!" cried Kingsly. "The information is already there." We raced to the opposite end of the lab and he pushed another button. Over the table top appeared a transparent grey cloud. As I watched, it thickened, assumed shape, and there was the cat, his legs just as they had been sprawled on the other table. The cat's chest moved, it completed the breath it had begun at the other end of the room!

Kingsly opened the receiver chamber, I entered and picked up the cat. My hands tingled, as if the sleeping animal were charged with static electricity.

We left the cat in his cage and Tiny took me on a tour of the rest of the laboratory. I saw the rock samples cored out of the earth by the disintegrator, and photographs taken through the deep earth probe of rock strata and molten magma. "All our original work was financed by a grant from the Mohole project," he told me. "They were, of course, very interested in getting samples back to the surface. Then, when we developed the laser beam method of sending from disintegrator to reintegrator, we tried to get the Space Agency to fund us. Seems like the obvious answer to interplanetary travel and——"

"Of course," I interrupted, excited by the prospect, "You could send supplies and equipment to the moon without rockets, instantaneously!"

He smiled at my enthusiasm. "Well, not quite," he replied. "You have to send the receiver-reintegrator unit up by rocket first. And then the transport is not instantaneous, it is restricted by the speed of light, plus the time it takes the reintegrator to put the object back together. That may not be much time, but when you are dealing with interplanetary distances and living beings, it may be crucial."

We were standing in the animal laboratory and I was suddenly so overwhelmed by the images his words had created in my mind that I sat down on top of the cage where the anesthetized tomcat still dozed undisturbed. "Wow," I breathed. I had a sudden vision of all the planets of the solar system, their satellites, their *artificial* satellites, interconnected by a web of laser beams, shipping supplies and astronauts from Earth to Jupiter, to Venus, even to remote Pluto. "The possibilities are fantastic. Living beings, you said, yes, living humans, that's the most important variable, isn't it?"

"Yes," replied Dr. Kingsly, "that's why we made the experimental set so large. To date, we haven't dared try it on anything but animals. I must confess, I thought it would work and be perfectly harmless, and it is a good thing Doc persuaded me to try it on mice. When those mice came through dead I realized how close I'd come to trying it on myself!" He laughed. "Since then I've been much more cautious."

"I can see your point," I said, "do you think it will be possible to send living humans through your laser beam apparatus?"

"Oh, yes, I still believe it can be done. I think we could do it safely now," he stated with more surety, "but after the rat experiment I promised Doc that we would go slow and be sure the thing was completely safe before using it on a man." He stood towering over me. "Come along," he said, "I'll show

11

you the rest of the lab and then you can pick up your specimens." He led me out of the laboratory where we had done the cat transmission experiment, past the atomic power plant to the other end of the building. Here in a large bare room were a few machines I did not recognize and one that I did— a large television receiver. Dr. Moritz and another man were in the room. Tiny took me around to the other side of the room and out into the courtyard beyond, pointing out the huge bundle of cables that ran from the drilling tower outside to the machines in the room.

"This is our deep probe," he announced with pride as we stood beside the scaffolding of the tower. There was a three foot wide depression in the asphalt pavement of the yard directly under the tower and by leaning over I could see that it funneled rapidly down to about a foot across. Suspended over the hole was a complex device on shock absorbers, mostly a metal enclosed box eight feet on a side. From this ran the cables to the receiver in the lab behind us. In the bright sunlight I could faintly see the reddish laser beam which extended down into the crater.

"Do you have a probe down there now?" I asked.

He nodded. "As deep as it has ever been," he said, almost in a whisper. I looked up at him. For the first time his face seemed lined and serious. "Deep, deep," he repeated, half to himself, "we are not really sure how deep. Nor do we know how long we can maintain contact with it. A slight shift in the earth's crust may cut off our laser beam and we'll lose contact."

Kingsly lowered his large frame onto part of the tower scaffold and leaned back against one of the uprights. "This is a far more elaborate experiment than we have tried before," he said. "It is a real test of the space station idea—we've sent down a probe which is both a disintegrator and a reintegrator. Then, through it we have sent automated television cameras and receivers as well as collection machinery and a power supply."

"You have?" I was amazed. "But where on earth did they go when they got there? Surely you can't materialize a television camera in solid rock!"

"No, no," he hastened to correct me, "that's true, but we found an open space in the crust, or rather under the crust. A big space—we really can't say how big—where we could maneuver the camera by remote control." I had a mental image of a black airless cavern miles beneath the surface of the earth, the probe breaking through, disgorging its reintegrator and materializing another set of machines to prowl through the dark, perhaps with their dim guide lights making weird shadows on rocky walls never seen by man. This image was in some ways correct, but also amazingly wrong.

"Through caverns measureless to man, down to a sunless sea," I quoted.

"True, true," said the big mathematician, jumping back to his feet, his good spirits quickly returning. He thumped me on the back—a blow that might have staggered a man who weighed less. "Come on," he said, "they're not measureless to man now, we're busy measuring them. Come back to the TV room and you can have a look at caverns undreamed of, more than 200 miles below the surface!"

I looked at the drilling tower and its laser machinery in amazement. "200 miles?"

"Well, that's our original estimate. Doc keeps recalculating the damn thing. I don't think he'll ever make up his mind."

Back inside the laboratory I watched the bare wall of the cave over Dr. Moritz's shoulders. "The walls are smooth lava," he said, "wait a moment and I'll sweep the camera around so you can see." He went to his control panel and made several adjustments. The cave wall began to move to the right on the screen. The rock was featureless, black. After a long half minute the camera picked up an utterly incongruous object. It appeared to be a shiny steel cylinder about 8 inches in diameter and over a foot long. It protruded through the floor of the rock chamber. From its top a beam of light fanned out to be dimly reflected from the cavern's roof. It was only then that it occurred to me that the television camera that was enabling me to see the underground scene must also be equipped with searchlights.

"That's the probe," said Tiny's voice behind me proudly. "What we've been seeing is being picked up by a mobile remote unit ten times its size we sent down the beam a day ago to explore."

"Can we see the remote?" I asked.

"No, it's not capable of turning its lens on itself. Here, come with me," he took my arm. "I'll show you another just like it."

We crossed the room and entered another storage area. In front of me crouched a thing only two feet high and three feet wide that looked like a toy tank. It had tank treads and rounded turret on top that glistened with recessed lenses I assumed were the lights of cameras.

"It looks like a toy," I said.

He laughed. "It is. That is, it was made for us by one of the local California toy companies. I'd show you how it works, but Doc has the only set of controls out there in the TV room." He paused a moment. "Well," he said, patting the top of the little mobile unit, "this is the one that made it. Let me show you some of our failures."

We went back into the main lab and into the other storeroom where Dr. Kingsly opened several freezers before he found what he wanted. "These are the mice and the rabbit used in the first experiments in the apparatus."

"Let's package them up and I'll take them back to the University for autopsy," I said, "I have stuff there for getting microscope slides made of all the organs—or even electron microscope pictures if it seems indicated." He found some paper sacks and we put the frozen animals in them. "Now I want to go collect that amazing cat I saw disintegrated and reconstituted," I said, but at that moment we were interrupted.

"Dr. Kingsly!" yelled one of the technicians, rushing into the room. "Dr. Kingsly, Dr. Moritz says come to the TV viewing room quick, there's something on the screen!"

We ran to the room. The large screen showed glistening rock walls, I could make nothing of it. "I'm here, Doc," said Kingsly at my elbow. Dr. Moritz did not take his eyes off the screen. With both hands he manipulated the knobs controlling the television monitor through whose electronic eye we were now gazing into the bowels of the earth.

"It's not visible now," said Moritz. "I've moved the mobile unit some distance down the passage and we've come to a larger chamber. I'm not sure how big it is. When I first came on it, though, I had the impression that something moved."

"Moved!" cried Kingsly, "My God, Doc, if there's any slippage of the rock it'll interrupt the laser beam and we'll lose contact with the probe and the remote!"

"I know, I know," the scientist muttered, "but the movement was on the other side of the cavern. Wait a minute, I'll see if I can get closer." He spun a dial and the passageway in front of the little TV tank appeared on the screen, startlingly bright in the glare of its searchlight.

The rocky floor gave way almost immediately into darkness the light beam did not penetrate. Across the screen there was a line, almost a knife edge of reflecting rock; beyond, only void.

Behind me Kingsly cursed, "You're on the edge of a precipice," he said. "No telling how deep it is. If you get any closer the tank will fall in and we may never get another look at anything. Try to both sides."

Dr. Moritz made the necessary adjustments, but as the view swept from side to side we could see that the edge of the cliff, if that is what it was, met the side walls of the tunnel on both sides. "We're stuck," he grunted.

I could visualize the tiny toy tank, its light beam thrusting into the impenetrable dark, sitting on the lip of some abysmal chasm hundreds of miles beneath us.

"Here's the opposite wall again," said Moritz, bringing it into focus. "It seems to be about a hundred yards away, and as you can see, there are passages leading out of it." Indeed there were several pitch black holes in the rock wall. "This is where I thought I saw movement."

"Sweep the beam downward, Doc," said Kingsly, "let's see how deep the chamber is on the opposite side."

The light beam began to descend. In fact, the rocky floor of the cave room came quickly into view, for the opposite wall was only about 30 feet high. But at that moment a gasp of astonishment went up from all of us within the room. There were several dark objects scattered on the floor of the cave casting inky shadows in the glare of the robot's searchlight. I assumed they were boulders, scattered by whatever volcanic convulsions of the subsurface had produced the tunnel, and indeed most of them were. But as the light beam touched the floor of the cave, one of these dark objects moved with incredible swiftness. It leaped from the floor, clung to the farther wall for a split second and then had scrambled up the rock and disappeared into a dark cave mouth. For the instant it was framed in the searchlight's beam, however, we all had time to clearly perceive its incredible nature.

It was a human being.

II

DOWN THE BEAM

Two weeks went by before anything moved in that black pit again. Doc had been recording everything that happened and he and Tiny went over and over the videotaped sequence. They learned very little more. The man appeared to be short and muscular and almost naked. Around his loins he wore a dark skirt-like garment. His face was never visible, his hair was long and dark. It was assumed he was a man and not a woman because of the obvious muscle development in arms and shoulders. He was barefoot. There were ornamental bracelets around one wrist and one ankle, and a necklace of some sort around his neck.

"Tiny, that beam must be bent." Dr. Moritz leaned his elbows on the table in their office. I'd heard them go over this argument before, and I knew what Dr. Kingsly's answer would be. "Doc, that's a laser out there," he gestured toward the window through which we could see the drilling tower and its enigmatic machinery crouched over the pavement. "That beam has got to be straight down. I still think it's possible we've gone clear through the earth."

"Not unless the planet's shaped like a disc," the little scientist snapped. "The time it takes to send a signal down and get a response back is compatible with a depth of 200 to 300 miles!"

"Unless the timing mechanism is faulty."

"I don't see how," Dr. Moritz replied. "I think we've angled the beam and come up somewhere in the Sierra Nevada mountains."

"Right," said Dr. Kingsly sarcastically, "and what was that thing we saw? The famous California Big Foot, no doubt! That beam is straight and it's straight down. Now I know light is deflected in a gravitational field but that's talking about the gravitational field of a star, not a puny little planet!"

"I agree," said Doc, serious again. They would go through this argument, yelling at each other, and then suddenly calm down and get very serious. "Now let's go over the possibilities again. One, the light beam of the laser has somehow been deflected and come to the surface a short distance away. This violates what we know about the straight line transmission of light."

"It's impossible," Kingsly grunted.

"Two," Moritz continued, ignoring him entirely for the moment, "the probe may have gone clear through the earth, although this seems unlikely unless the earth is different in shape from what we believe it to be."

"Impossible," Kingsly agreed.

"Then," the scientist went on, "we are the victims

18

of an elaborate hoax, equipment failure or hallucination."

"Hoax and equipment failure are out," said Kingsly, "too many good technicians have gone over the equipment. It's working the way it's supposed to. Hallucination is out. Video tape doesn't have hallucinations. We've shown that tape to the lab people who weren't here when cave-man Joe appeared. They all see him as clear as we do."

Dr. Moritz turned to me and shrugged his shoulders. "Every possibility seems to violate some law of nature as we presently understand it. That may be necessary, of course, but first I want to consider every alternative explanation."

"I've got another," I said.

"Let's have it," said Kingsly. "It can't be any more improbable than the ones we've got."

"There are people living 200 miles below the earth's crust," I said.

"Nope," said Dr. Kingsly after a polite moment's consideration, "the pressure is too great for life to exist at such a depth, except maybe microbes."

"Wait a minute, Doc," said Tiny Kingsly. "The cavern itself is an impossibility at that depth, isn't it?"

"Probably, which would only prove that we are really at the surface. No, I think gas vapor under tremendous pressure could produce the caves we've seen."

"OK," said Kingsly, "then how about measuring the pressure? We should be able to devise a telemetry gadget. . . ." They were off again, heads together, minds racing, having just seen a new twist to their problem. It occurred to me that we might try to guess where the probe had come up and locate it by radio signal location, but then I remembered that the two scientists thought it might be anywhere from China to the nearby California mountains.

One of the laboratory technicians stuck his head through the door. "Come quick, Dr. Moritz, lights are moving on the screen." We ran.

There was no doubt about it, there were lights in the mouth of the cave through which our mysterious troglodyte had disappeared two weeks before. They looked like flames and when Doc got them into focus we could see that they were torches in the hands of about a dozen people standing close to the lip of the larger chamber.

"I can't see them clearly," Tiny hissed, "turn on the searchlights!"

"Fool," Moritz answered, "you want to scare them away? I'm not going to do anything. It's their move now. Has somebody got the recorder running?"

"Sure thing, Doc," came a voice from behind us.

The torches flickered in the blackness. The little group at the far side of the cave did not approach any closer. Perhaps they were afraid. The time seemed to drag on interminably.

"I wish we had audio!" Kingsly burst out. "They might be trying to talk to us."

"Well, we had no way of knowing we were going to want to hear as well as see," Moritz snapped. "Design a microphone pickup for the other tank and we'll send it down!" Kingsly only grunted, and he did not, of course, set off immediately on this new errand.

Suddenly there was a stir among the figures on the television screen. A large object appeared among them, was raised momentarily over their heads and then cast into the cave in the direction of the TV tank. Moritz switched on the searchlight and swept the beam across the floor to find the motionless, tumbled form.

"What is it?" "Some kind of animal!" "Something in a sack!" Our speculations filled the room while Doc struggled to get better illumination and focus.

"There!" he exclaimed finally, "That's the best I can do. Now what do you think it is?"

"A dead beast," Tiny Kingsly's voice rose over the noise of the rest of us. "Some kind of antelope, I would guess, I don't recognize it. Quite dead and the carcass cleaned, you can see part of the incision on the belly. Don't you agree, Chris?"

"Yes," I answered, "it's obviously the body of some animal, partially butchered. You can see the hoofs and the antlers. But why did they throw it at the TV pickup?"

"I'll tell you why," said Moritz. "I think it is a sacrifice." He swung the camera's lens back to focus on the cave mouth where the group of men had been standing. They were gone.

After that I was very busy for several days in the animal lab. When I got back to the earth probe experimental station the situation had changed again.

"They've built a kind of altar in the center of the large cavern," said Dr. Moritz, focusing the TV screen for me. It did look like an altar, or rather a large stone table almost as high as a man. The top was a solid slab of stone.

"Where did they find that piece that's on top?"

"They carried it in on their backs," Moritz answered. "They're amazingly organized and strong but they seem to have no technology at all. They did that building job without levers or wheels, and see, they've built a set of steps down into the cave on their side."

"What do they look like?" I asked, "Can you identify them yet?"

"We've got some stuff on video tape. Here, let me show you." He turned to the technician behind him, "Take over the monitor for a moment, Bob."

We left the big TV screen room and entered a smaller lab where, with some difficulty, Dr. Moritz got a small TV screen going and showed me the tapes of the cavemen building their stone artifacts.

"They're all men," I commented.

"Right, we've seen no women. The men are all hairy, bearded and poorly dressed," he replied. "As far as we can tell, they are dressed only in animal skins, we've seen nothing that looks like cloth. Or metal either," he added. "Their tools and weapons —they usually carry their spears and knives with them, are all wood and stone."

"A Stone Age culture," I mused, "Where on the face of the earth are people still living in the stone age? New Guinea?"

Dr. Moritz rubbed his beard with his hand thoughtfully. "I doubt it," he said, "No tattooing, the weapons seem too crude. A Stone Age culture, to be sure, but where?"

"The mountains of Tibet?" I suggested wildly.

"No," he answered, "I doubt it. When Tiny gets his new gadgets together we can send down the sound pickup and hear their language. Then we'll get some anthropologists in and identify them. I've been afraid to do that yet—the whole story seems so impossible." He sat for a while, chin in hand, watching the enigmatic figures on the TV screen. It seemed paradoxical that this miracle of modern electronics should bewilder us by producing images that might easily have been our own prehistoric ancestors.

"Stone Age culture," Dr. Moritz said again, "but where? It's a lost world."

I interrupted. "Where is Tiny—I mean Dr.

Kingsly? I've got some animals out in the truck I want him to transmit for me."

We went in search of the huge scientist and he hastened to help me get my specimens.

"Quick work, Chris," he said, as we brought the cages into the laboratory.

"Not really," I answered. "I've pulled all the experimental animals I can get off of other projects. This matter transmitter thing seems more important to me, and I got my boss to agree. These animals have been trained in a whole variety of tasks, maze running, lever pressing, symbol discrimination, timing tests and everything. I've even included my own favorite subject, Pinky, the big tomcat with the metal plate in the top of his head—he's wired so that I can record his brain waves."

"Good," said Kingsly, "now you handle the anesthesia and I'll guarantee to disintegrate each of your animals before your very eyes and bring them back alive!"

We began the long task of preparing each of the experimental animals for the matter transmitter, running it through the machine and having it rematerialize on the other side of the room. Each of them then had to be revived and put back in their cages for the trip back to the University. It was late in the day when I got my charges back to the animal lab and many days before I finished testing them. The test results were sufficiently encouraging, and my curiosity about what was going on at the other end of the earth probe was sufficiently strong, that I drove out to Santa Monica again to report in person.

I sat with the two scientists in the conference room where we had met before. The blackboard was covered with equations I could not understand, and the table itself was littered with parts for Kingsly's audio probe device, but they listened to me with quiet interest.

"You conclude then, Chris," Dr. Moritz said when I had finished, "that all your animal subjects are well, both physically and psychologically?"

"Yes, indeed," I replied, "not only that, the rat data indicates the animals are more intelligent than before they went through the matter transmitter!"

"Hah!" shouted Kingsly in delight, "you see—not only harmless, it's good for them!"*

"And you?" I questioned. "How far have you gotten in identifying your mysterious following of cave men?"

"Strangely enough," said Dr. Moritz, "we have gotten nowhere. We have two TV pickups down there now, and the microphone."

"Don't think they didn't go wild when the second unit showed up!" commented Kingsly, "they thought their mechanical god had sent to heaven for his brother. When those two searchlights went on together they cheered and chanted like crazy."

"But," said Dr. Moritz, "we are no nearer to identifying them than we were before. I have played tape recordings of their speech for several anthropologists and none of them can identify their language. Meanwhile, we are learning a little of it, although mostly the names of animals they bring in as sacrifices."

"Animals?" I said. "What kinds of animals? Surely we can identify the country by the species of wild animals they come up with."

"I doubt it," said Kingsly, "three or four kinds

* Editor's note: Christopher West was mistaken about this, although he had no way of knowing about it at the time. These exepriments with the rats have been repeated several times since his departure, and this initial improvement has proven to be a chance variation in test scores.

24

of antelope, some monkeys, a large sloth-like creature and a kind of bull. Nothing that helps identify the area at all."

At this moment we were interrupted by the buzzing of the telephone set on the conference table. Further speculation was quickly abandoned when Dr. Moritz turned to us after answering, "Something new on the screen," he said briefly.

This time when we burst into the laboratory room the screen was filled with the images of the cave people. All were men, and a more ugly, unpleasant-looking crowd I have never seen. They were long-haired and bearded and their bodies were covered with shaggy hair. Each wore a loincloth of animal fur, some with the tails or paws hanging nearly to the ground. They were grouped behind the stone altar, facing towards us. Their grinning faces were illuminated by a fire before the stone altar as well as torches scattered around the cave. Directly in front of them a man stood at the end of the altar, his hands raised over his head in supplication. He was clad in the most amazing outfit I had ever seen. Over his head was fitted the skull and antlers of some animal like a large elk. This bizarre headdress fitted on the top of his head like a hat. The skin of the animal fell down over his back like a cape. Over each of his hands he had fitted the paws of some clawed animal like a bear so that the furred sleeves reached up to his elbows and the clawed hands glittered in the torchlight. He was not looking toward us but at the other three figures standing before the altar.

Indeed, these three figures dominated the scene and drew every eye in the room. Two men and a woman—they stood there, defiant, obviously prisoners, bound with coil after coil of what looked like a vine or rawhide rope. All three were naked, obviously stripped of their weapons, ornaments and clothing by their captors. The two men were tall, taller than our cave men, strong, unafraid. One was older, by his white hair and beard, the other young, the dried blood of a recent wound disfiguring his face. The girl was unbelievable. Never have I seen a creature so beautiful. Her hair was black and fell in a wild tangle to her waist. Her eyes were large and filled with fear and bravery. Her nude body was slender and magnificent in the firelight.

She turned her gaze toward the fantastically garbed priest as he began to chant. The crowd answered him with a deep throated yell of bloodthirsty ferocity.

"My God," gasped Kingsly at my elbow, "they're going to sacrifice them, Doc! Do something!"

"There's nothing I can do," Moritz cried, "we have no real way to communicate with them. The tanks are trapped on top of their ledge."

"Dr. Kingsly," I said, grabbing him by the arm. "Listen, listen to me!" The sound of the primitives' chant filled the room. Kingsly's eyes were glued to the screen of the giant TV set. The high priest shouted an order drowned in the noise. Two warriors leaped forward. They seized the younger prisoner by the elbows and raised him to the top of the stone altar.

"There's nothing we can do, Chris," Kingsly muttered. "There's no way to stop them."

"Yes, there is!" I cried, "You've got to send me down the beam!"

His head turned then and his eyes met mine. I think he read the resolve in my face for he took me very seriously. "We don't know that it's safe," he began.

"Yes it is," I argued, in desperation, "the animals are well. You know you can do it. It's the only possible way to communicate with them! We've got to risk it!" My gaze strayed back to the screen. The beautiful black-haired girl stood tall in her bonds, her horrified gaze fixed on the man now stretched on the altar. "Quick, Tiny, before it's too late!"

"Do you really want to risk it, Chris?"

"Yes, yes, let's get moving!"

"I don't know if we can get you back again." He hesitated yet another moment and our eyes turned up to the barbaric spectacle on the screen. The high priest raised a huge stone knife in both hands and brought it down with a wild shout on the chest of the human sacrifice. The dying man cried out involuntarily. The girl swayed as if she was going to faint but then regained her feet. A gasp of horror went up from the observers in the room.

"Quick, Tiny," I cried, "we may be able to save the girl!" He took another look at my face and then turned, quickly, to accompany me.

"Into the lab at the end of the corridor!" he cried. "We'll risk it if you dare!" We left the room at a run.

"Have you got a gun?" I asked. It suddenly had occurred that I was going to confront fifty savages with my bare hands.

"There's nothing like that in the building," said Dr. Kingsly, stopping for a moment. "No, it wouldn't be safe. The ammunition could explode during the disintegration process. Do you have a knife?"

"No," I said, thrusting my hands into my pockets, "nothing."

"Here," he handed me a jackknife he pulled from his pants pocket, then turned and darted into another room. It was an electronic laboratory, the walls hung with spools and springs of wire. "There must be something you can use," he said.

"Oh, come on," I argued, "we haven't got time."

As he came back out into the hall, Kingsly stopped in front of a cabinet set into the wall. The word FIRE was painted on the glass door in large letters. "Wait a moment," he said. He opened the door and reached inside. Beside a coiled hose was an axe in a bracket. He pulled it loose and handed it to me. I hefted the weapon. The handle was three feet long, the head flattened into a hammer on one end, sharpened to a good edge on the other. The axe head and part of the handle were painted bright red. I hefted the unlikely weapon for a moment, little guessing what a profound influence it was to have over my future. Then Kingsly and I hurried into the next laboratory.

The disintegrator unit dominated the room. The giant projector loomed over it. The rest of the room was filled with carefully labeled boxes shelved on three of the four walls and piled together on the floor. Each contained a sample of rock brought up during the initial descent of the earth probe. A giant snake of cables led from the disintegrator unit out through a hole cut in the wall to the laser unit at the drilling tower. Dr. Kingsly opened one end of the disintegration chamber and I crawled in on my hands and knees.

"Wait," he said, "My God, what about the anesthetic?"

"Forget the anesthetic, Kingsly," I pleaded, "there isn't time. I'd never wake up in time to save those poor victims. Go ahead and shoot!"

He hesitated another moment and then bent to speak to me through the chamber door. "Lie down on your side," he said. "Don't move if you can help it. You'll arrive in the cave behind the TV cameras and it will be dark. That will give you a few moments to prepare yourself. We think they call their god Tanak-Ah. Shout that out—they may take you for an incarnation of the god himself. Good-by and good luck." He slammed the door and I could no longer hear him. I lay down on my right side so I could watch him through the glass. He hurried to the controls of the machine and set several dials. A warning light went on above the panel in front of him. He looked up at me a moment. His finger touched a button.

I felt a sheet of flame descend over the left side of my chest and envelop my body. I lost consciousness.

III

THE BATTLE IN THE CAVE

When I came to my senses I was still lying on my right side. It was dark but not pitch black and as I moved to sit up, I saw the flickering light of flames somewhere down the corridor. The cave roof was lower than I had thought—I could not stand upright. I flexed my muscles and shifted the axe from hand to hand. Everything seemed to be working okay. The terrible pain was gone. I had made it, I was the first human being to be laser-transported by the Moritz-Kingsly process! A burst of yelling from the distant cavern cut short my self-congratulation and reminded me of my urgent errand. Half crouching I ran down the passageway to come suddenly on one of the small self-propelled TV units. The operator of the unit must have spotted me, for the little device immediately turned and rolled ahead of me to the point where the passage opened into the larger cave.

The scene that met my eyes was enough to make the hair stand up on the back of my neck. The torches glowed off the rocky walls and the low roof. Immediately in front of me was the stone altar. Both the male prisoners lay upon it in gory death. I had arrived too late to save the second man. Between them lay the bound naked body of the girl. For an instant I thought she too had been butchered, but then I saw that the chest between those magnificent breasts was intact. She turned her head slightly toward me to look up, not at me, for I was still unnoticed, but at the eerie figure of the antlered, half-beastial form of the priest who leaned over her, holding the dripping, blood-smeared, sacrificial stone knife. Sizzling in the stone brazier at the side of the altar were two blackened lumps of tissue that I recognized as the actual hearts of the two previous victims.

Behind this horrid tableau massed some thirty or more of the fur-clad savages, their eyes glinting in the firelight, their hairy faces, barbaric ornaments and stone-tipped weapons flashing in the light of the flames. Here I stood, a typical twentieth century man, armed only with a fire axe, pitted against a room full of Stone Age savages.*

*Editor's note: Chris West's characterization of himself as a "typical twentieth century man" is so inaccurate that I must give the reader the picture of him which he is obviously never going to provide. Mr. West was endowed with a magnificent physique as well as an intelligent brain. In college he played football for two years until he decided it interfered with his pre-medical studies. He stood 6 feet 6 inches tall and habitual exercise had kept him in excellent shape. He was a surfer and a diver. At this time he weighed about one hundred and eighty pounds, none of which was excess fat. His subsequent adventures in the lost world caused him to lose some weight and become more wiry but did not alter his general proportions. In addition to his physical condition, he was a veteran of four

As I saw the priest raise his grisly knife over the fair form of the maiden whose plight had brought me 200 miles through the surface of the earth, I rose to my feet.

"Tanak-Ah!" I cried, my voice echoing in the rocky cavern. I stood, holding the red-bladed axe over my head in both hands. The searchlights of both TV units were turned to illuminate me. The effect was electric. Every face in the room turned toward me and a momentary silence fell as the cave men ceased their chanting in amazement. Then the spell broke. I don't know what went through the high priest's mind. Perhaps he saw whatever power he held over his people being snatched away from him. Perhaps he was blood-crazed by the preceding murders. Anyway, he turned back to the petrified girl and raised the knife over her with both hands.

"Strike not! The Gods forbid it!" I shouted, but the weapon began to descend on her defenseless breast. I leaped from my ledge and landed on the

---

years in the Marine Corps. As a civilized man, I regret the need for our young men to spend part of their lives learning to take the lives of others, but there is little doubt that in his present circumstances this training has accounted to a considerable extent to his continued survival. Physical violence and, in all probability, hand-to-hand combat, was not unfamiliar to him, at any rate. The academic training he had received in the biological and medical sciences however, did him little good, I fear. At the moment he was sent down the beam, Chris West was 25 years old. He was a big man, clean shaven but with his blond hair cut long in the current style so that ends of it swept his shoulders. When he entered the matter transmitter he was wearing Indian moccasins, singularly appropriate for his new surroundings. He was otherwise dressed in blue jeans and a grey sweatshirt with the letters of the University of Southern California printed on the front of it in red. In Los Angeles his appearance, except for his size, would have attracted little attention. In the primitive world he had entered, it was startlingly unusual.

opposite side of the altar. As I did so, I brought the axe down on that antlered headdress with all the force I could muster. The blade smashed through his head down to the level of his eyes and he fell forward over the body of his intended victim.

I wrenched the axe free and pitched the corpse of the high priest backward off the girl. Seizing the sacrificial knife I cut the rawhide ropes which were wound around her body and which lashed her hands behind her. Holding my axe in my right hand I raised her up with my left arm and lifted her off the altar.

So far the savages had not moved. I hoped they were paralyzed with superstitious fear, but probably they were just dumbfounded. I set the girl on her feet. She seemed unhurt. She was rubbing her arms and hands to get the circulation back. She spoke to me in a soft voice, but, of course, I could not understand a word she said.

A murmur began in the crowd. Those in the rear seemed to be urging some course of action on the front ranks which they, quite evidently, were reluctant to follow. I could see that the girl and I were very likely to be in big trouble. I hefted my axe and picked up the stone knife and handed it to her. She was a cool one! She took the knife with a brief word and stepped behind me to my right. Together we faced the throng. The altar and its attendant braziers made a barrier before us, but there was open space on either side. I glanced behind me. The wall of the cave was only six feet away. The opening of the tunnel guarded by the two TV tanks was about four feet above our heads, but to gain that relative shelter we would have to turn our backs to our enemies.

The shouting in the back of the cave became

louder and more imperative and those in front answered back in harsh voices. I could easily imagine the nature of the argument. Those in back were insisting that I was a stranger, an interloper in the sacred temple, and that I should be dealt with accordingly, probably summarily executed. Those in front were protesting that I might indeed be the supernatural being my sudden apparition suggested and, as such, should be treated with at least a minimum of respect. The argument waxed hot, but the savages began to surge forward towards us. It appeared that the conservative viewpoint was going to prevail, as is so often the case. I tried desperately to think of some miraculous stunt I could pull off, but my mind was a blank. Apparently my slaughter of the high priest was not adequate proof of my supernatural origin.

Angry faces shouted at me, and, getting no answer, advanced, brandishing stone-tipped spears. Fortunately, no one attempted to cast a spear at me, as it is unlikely I could have dodged in that narrow space. A large man with broken teeth rushed at me, his face contorted in a fierce grimace. Holding the axe in both hands I managed to deflect his spear thrust, and, as he lunged toward me, chopped down on him, smashing his right shoulder so that his weapon fell clattering to the floor. He leaped back, screaming, his left hand holding his wound. The others pressed forward and I prepared to sell my life as dearly as possible when suddenly the illumination in the cave changed dramatically. The cave men halted, gasping with astonishment. Both the searchlights above my head had begun a rapid flickering, sweeping back and forth across the crowd.

The result, in the darkened cave, where the torches and fires gave little light anyway, was a bizarre strobe effect. There was a murmur of awe, and some of the savages began to turn to run up the steps on the far side of the rock walled room. Indeed, I could see a retreat beginning up the steps and out the far passage. With a great cry of triumph I sprang forward, brandishing my axe, and cleared a space around the altar. Then I turned and, reaching up, snatched one of the tank-like mobile units off its ledge and set it on the rocky floor. Immediately it rushed at the nearest group of natives, its searchlight flashing menacingly. Somebody on the surface was thinking fast and furiously.*

Now a shout of real fear went up, from those close enough to see this new menace. I quickly plucked the second unit down and set it also on the floor. A few spears hit the wall over my head, but the attackers were hindered by the need to cast over the heads of their companions who were fighting their way back to the exit. In a few minutes the room was cleared except for the girl and myself and the three dead men. The shouting and screaming of the frightened savages still echoed from the far cave, however, and I did not think we had won more than a brief respite. Our immediate need was to escape from the cave, preferably to the surface. I turned to my beautiful companion.

"Out," I said, gesturing, "out and up if there's a way!"

She nodded her head and reached out her left hand, took hold of mine. Pulling me behind her, she began a quick rush across the cave.

"Doc, Tiny," I yelled over my shoulder as I followed her up the stone steps, "I've got to get her out of here before they get up nerve enough to come back for us!"

We entered the cave mouth and made a quick turn to the left. Immediately it was pitch black and

*Editor's note: It was Dr. Moritz.

we slowed to a walk. My lovely guide kept hold of my hand and felt her way along the cave wall with her other hand, in which she still held the stone knife. Suddenly we came into a larger cave in the center of which burned a small cooking fire. Gathered about it were several unkempt women, no better dressed than the men I had seen. But I had no eyes for them, for on the far side of the cave was an opening, half-way up the wall, through which I could see a patch of daylight!

The girl at my side whispered to me, pointing to the cave entrance. I could see now that a steep path led up from the floor of the cave to our destination. I nodded, turned to look at her. Her beautiful lips parted in a brief smile and she turned back to the cave. I started across the larger cave at a trot, the girl close at my heels. The women around the fire caught sight of us and fled shrieking, snatching up several small children who were crawling on the floor nearby. I ignored them, they were no threat, and we gained the bottom of our path to freedom unopposed. My hopes were soon dashed, however. The light above was momentarily darkened. I looked up and saw two men framed in the cave mouth. As their eyes grew used to the dark they saw me climbing up toward them and came down on me with a shout. They must have been lounging outside the cave entrance and the screams of the women had brought them in. One carried only a stone knife, but the other pulled from a thong loop at his waist a great stone-headed hammer or war axe. He leaped down the slope toward me, whirling this deadly weapon around his head. I wasted no breath, for I was running uphill. I rushed in faster than he expected, under his guard, and hit him with a bone jarring body block. He was only stunned for a moment, but that was enough.

Dropping my fire axe at my feet I heaved the body of my antagonist up over my head to hurtle down the slope to the bottom of the cave. I turned to seek the second man, grabbing up my axe as I did. A shout of rage burst from me as I did so, for the cowardly savage had attacked the girl. She had managed to get hold of the wrist of his knife hand but he was clutching at her other hand, which held her own knife, and at the same time dragging her closer up the rocky slope. He turned as I cried out, but I gave him no time to respond. Reversing the axe in my hand I struck him at the temple with the flat hammer end of the steel blade. His grip on the girl's arm loosened instantly and he toppled at our feet.

"Kree-gah!" she said, pointing upward.

"You said it, baby," I replied, "let's kree-gah out of here before anybody else shows up." We hastened up the path and burst out of the cave into brilliant sunlight.

For a moment I was dazzled, and my companion took me by the hand again and led me down a path away from the cave mouth. My first impression of the inner world was one of blazing greens and blues. The colors seemed particularly intense and the light and heat of the sun overpowering. When I could appreciate the view I caught my breath in amazement.

We were high up on the sheer face of a mountain, a narrow path led away to our right where, in the distance, the mountain seemed to tumble into lower, green hills. To the left, green cliffs stretched away as far as I could see. The tops of those cliffs were frequently covered with white clouds, though in places I could see saw-tooth ridges through the cloud. All were clothed in dense greenery, and at the foot of the cliffs below us, some thousands of feet down, I saw a thick green jungle. Masses of foliage covered the ground, broken here and there by the bare stalks of tall palms or by small grassy clearings. In these latter were herds of grazing animals which I could not identify in the distance. Several miles away the jungle ended in a bright yellow beach at the edge of a blue sea. The sea was brilliant, and studded with small green islands. In the distance the sea and sky seemed to fade one into the other without forming a clear horizon. A brisk breeze blew in from that beautiful ocean, and our perch on the mountain path was cool and windy despite a blazing noon-day sun directly overhead. In all that vast panorama of mountains, jungle and sea I could see no sign of the works of man. No ship sailed that azure ocean, no roof top or cleared field broke the expanse of greenery below us. The path we trod looked more appropriate to mountain goats than men. The air was free of aircraft. There were birds, to be sure, birds in great numbers. Flocks of white sea birds circled the air over the beach and off to the left I could see some great flying creatures soaring majestically back and forth across the face of the cliffs.

This was my introduction to the wild untamed beauty of Pellucidar.

I might have stood there like a tourist, gawking at the scenery, if my female companion had not pulled me by the hand, urging me to follow her down the path. Realizing the wisdom of putting as much distance as possible between ourselves and the tribe of outraged cave dwellers we had just left, I followed her naked form down the path. She was amazing! Barefoot and clad only in the black hair that flowed around her shoulders, still holding the big stone knife in her left hand, she led me along that narrow rocky trail through the Mountains of

Rains at a pace that was almost a trot. Not only that, she kept it up for what seemed hours, although to my surprise the sun did not seem to move in the sky. Gradually the trail led downward and finally entered thickly wooded hills far from where we had emerged from the ground. Here she finally stopped to rest where a tiny stream, descending from the heights above us, crossed the trail and continued to the left on its way to the sea. We crouched side by side and drank. I could see the girl was still wary, her eyes continually roamed the green vastness around us. I assumed that she feared pursuit by her previous captors. I did not yet know how filled with dangers was my new world. Every tree that overhung the trail, every turn, every clump of low greenery held, for my companion, the threat of sudden death. I was still telling myself that I was somewhere in Africa or South America, although the total absence of any sign of civilization puzzled me considerably. I was totally unable to account for the appearance of our late enemies, who under their hair and dirt appeared to have white skins, or for that matter, for the girl, who was obviously white skinned under a tan that showed a total disregard for clothes.

She noticed my fascinated appraisal of her and smiled again. She was obviously unembarrassed to have me staring at her naked body as she squatted comfortably beside the trail.

"Chris," I said, pointing to myself.

"Var-na," she replied, indicating herself.

"I'm delighted to meet you, Var-na," I said. "I assume that you are familiar enough with our present environment to know where the hell we are going?"

The dark-haired, dark-eyed beauty burst into merry laughter. Strangely enough, however, she

38

seemed to catch some of my meaning, for she then proceeded to answer my question. She picked up a stick and made a small hole in the soft mud beside the stream. "Had-bar," she said, gesturing back up the trail. Obviously this represented the cave from which we had escaped. Had-bar was the name of the tribe, although at the time I thought it might be the place. Varna traced a line with her stick, pointing to the two of us. "Varna, Chris," she said, pronouncing my name carefully, "Chris-No-hajdak," pointing to my axe, which lay beside me. I didn't know it then, but I had just been given my Pellucidarian name, Red Axe. Varna traced the course of our flight on the ground with her stick. She indicated a point along the line to be the stream where we presently sat. Our destination was some five times distant and was called Val-an. This was actually both the name of her tribe and of its territory or hunting grounds.

"Kree-gah," said my pretty guide, regaining her feet. We were under the shadows of the huge jungle trees now and she shivered a bit, rubbing her shoulders with her hands. I suddenly realized how impolite it was of me to remain clothed while she was naked. I pulled off my sweatshirt, now stained with dirt and blood, and offered it to her. She accepted with a pretty gesture and after a moment's trial and error, pulled it on over her head. In a moment her merry laugh burst forth again as she held up her arms to me. The sleeves of the sweater came down a good six inches past her hands. We hacked through the upper sleeves with the stone knife and left Varna with a somewhat serviceable garment which fell about her hips, leaving slender brown legs uncovered. She seemed delighted with the result, inspecting herself in a still pool beside the stream with all the posturing and re-arrangement of her hair a young woman on the outer surface might put into trying on a new dress in the department store.

"There's no doubt that you are the prettiest thing in this primeval forest, my dear," I said, "although that shirt is a bit too short, especially when you bend over like that."

She laughed again, picked up her knife in her left hand and caught my hand in her right. I carried my axe ready in case we should meet more of the Had-bar people, and hand in hand we walked on through that luxuriant jungle. As we walked, Varna undertook to teach me her language. I struggled hard to master it, for I wanted more than anything else to improve my communication with this lovely creature. She was every inch of her a female, but withal lithe and quick as a cat. In several places the path came upon deep narrow gullies crossed by the rotting trunks of fallen trees, covered with a growth of vines. Varna skipped along these precarious bridges as if she were light as a feather. She laughed at my obvious discomfort, racing ahead and waiting impatiently for me to catch up.

A few miles farther on we came upon a forest of bamboos. Varna stopped and explained to me, mostly by vigorous pantomine, that she wanted me to cut down several stalks and make them into spears about six feet long. I selected a few stout straight lengths of the bamboo and quickly chopped them down with my axe and trimmed them to length. Then I took out the pocket knife Dr. Kingsly had given me and whittled the ends into sharp points. Varna was delighted with the knife and inspected it very carefully. I could see that metal was new to her and correctly guessed that her own people, like her captors, were still in the

Stone Age. I tried to give her the knife but she refused and watched me put it back in my pocket. This process amused her immensely and I had to do it several times, taking the knife out and putting it back while she sat under the bamboos convulsed with laughter. I later discovered that the only creature she knew who had a pocket such as mine was a kind of kangaroo. The comparison tickled her sense of the ridiculous. I finally pulled the pocket of my pants inside out to demonstrate to her. She then acknowledged, by gestures again, that her people used such things, but on a strap around the shoulder or the waist. When I replaced the pocket she had to try putting her hands into it, a pleasantry I found absolutely delightful and which set her off into a train of giggles. Pulling her hands out of my pockets, she threw her arms around my shoulders and gave me an impulsive hug. A moment later she pulled away and became serious again, pointing down the trail. I nodded agreement and, picking up our bamboo spears, we continued on our way.

We must have walked for hours through that beautiful forest, but the sun never seemed to set. Occasionally it was obscured by the dense net of foliage overhead where the great trees soared up for hundreds of feet. Later, however, we would come to clearings where I could see the brilliant orb still directly overhead. There were birds in that forest and some tiny antelope, one of which Varna downed with a skillful cast of her spear and quickly dispatched with the stone knife. She indicated that we would soon come to a place where it was safe to rest and I shouldered the carcass of her kill and carried it with us. There were other animals around us but they were wary, and although I heard movements in the underbrush I saw nothing but their

41

tracks. So far I had recognized nothing that would tell me what part of the world the disintegrator-reintegrator had projected me to.

I wondered what my friends back in California were doing. Surely they would understand that my first duty was to see the girl safely back to her own people. After that I would have to figure out some way to get back into the cave and communicate with them. How I was going to do that I didn't know. I was certainly persona-non-grata with the cave people at the moment, having killed their high priest and put at least three more of them out of action. It would probably not be necessary to go back to the cave, however, I reassured myself. We were obviously going to Varna's people and some-one there would know how to reach civilization. Perhaps I was even now only a few miles from a radio station. I would quickly contact Dr. Moritz and Dr. Kingsly. I started to compose an appropriate message in my mind. Something like: "Congratulations on successful human disintegrator transport. Made the trip in good shape. Presently stranded in Amazon jungle. Please send funds for return journey."

At that moment something happened that put all thoughts of telegrams out of my mind forever. Varna halted in the trail, motioning me to caution. As I came quickly up beside her I saw to my amazement that she was sniffing the air! I sniffed myself but my smog-dulled sense of olfaction brought me no information. "What is it?" I whispered. Then there leaped into the path before us the most terrifying apparition I had ever seen in my short life. My first impression was of a huge cat, for the beast was six feet long and four feet high at its powerful shoulders. It was covered with a tawny fur. A stump of tail lashed the air behind it and huge claws were unsheathed on each of the massive forepaws. It was the head that was incredible, however. Ears back, the feline features were contorted in a fierce snarl. From the bared upper jaw descended two enormous scythe-like fangs, each at least a foot long. I knew immediately what it was that confronted us, although until that moment I would have sworn that no living man had ever seen one. I have stood as a child in Los Angeles' Rancho La Brea Park and gazed in fascination at the life-like statues there, and I recognized the beastial engine of destruction that now crouched before me.

It was a sabre-toothed tiger.

IV

VARNA'S TRIBE

The huge sabre-tooth crouched in the trail, studying us. The brilliant sun of the inner world filtered through the leaves of the bamboo forest and covered him with black and yellow stripes of light until he looked like his cousin of the outer surface. He was a magnificent beast, but I was ill prepared to appreciate his beauty. My previous experience with tigers had been entirely from the other side of a protective moat at the San Diego Zoo. I felt the cold sweat of fear start from my arm pits as I gazed into that savage maw. The beast snarled.

I slowly lowered the tip of my pitiful bamboo spear until it was leveled at my enemy. "Varna," I whispered, "run. Trees." There was no reply, but I did not hear her move. I dared not turn my head to look back at her. I felt if I took my eyes off the monster for a moment he would charge. I was certain the brave girl was still with me, but my small vocabulary in her language did not allow me to argue with her.

The sabre-tooth crouched lower to the ground and a fierce rumbling roar began from deep in his chest. Then to my terror and amazement he sprang the ten foot distance between us. I barely had time to lift my spear—the sharpened tip of it took him in the throat, the force of the great cat impaling himself on my lance threw me to the ground. The bamboo pole broke in two. The shriek of the sabre-tooth made the wood hideous. I rolled into the underbrush and scrambled to my feet, drawing my axe from my belt.

The tiger was still on his feet, the broken bamboo pole sticking through his throat. His horrid muzzle was red with blood. Confronting him, feet braced apart, spear held ready and level, was my darling Varna. The beast made a short rush at her, she stabbed at his face, and retreated down the trail. I was horrified at the danger she was in. The tiger seemed to be badly wounded, but he was paying no more attention to it than if he had had a toothpick stuck in his cheek. I rushed up behind him and swung the axe at his back as if I were trying to chop a fallen tree trunk. There was another hideous scream from the tiger. I had made a lucky stroke, my axe was buried in his back but it had severed his spinal cord, rendering his hind legs paralyzed. He turned and struck at me with one of those huge forepaws, but fortunately the stick in his neck got in his way and I leaped back to safety.

I thought now our enemy was disabled and probably dying, but I reckoned without the incredible vitality of prehistoric life. The sabre-tooth had now definitely identified me as his principal antagonist. My broken spear was sticking through his neck and my axe was buried in his back, the handle protruding up through the tawny fur. The beast was choking on his own blood and his hind legs were useless but he was deliberately and rapidly crawling toward me, snarling defiance.

Varna raced up behind him and began jabbing at the back of his head with her spear until he turned and started toward her. "The axe!" she cried, in her own tongue. I recognized the word and, while the beast was engaged in trying to reach and rend my lady friend with his claws, I yanked the axe free from his spine. Either he didn't feel it because of his injured spinal cord or was too enraged by Varna's dancing just out of reach in front of him, for he kept crawling towards her. This enabled me to come up behind his head and bring the steel bladed axe down on the back of his skull with all the force I could muster. The great cat gave one final roar of defiance and slumped, head down between his huge forepaws, the mighty sabre teeth buried in the dirt.

Varna rushed to me, touching me to be sure I was unharmed, shamelessly hugging me and cooing her delight at our narrow escape. And narrow indeed it had been. The tarag, as she called it, was rightfully feared by her tribe, a crafty, powerful beast with the habit of killing lonely hunters or children of the tribe. Varna left me to jump up upon the dead carcass where she executed a dance of triumph. This completed, she retrieved my axe and, motioning me to help her, rolled the huge beast over and began to skin it with the stone knife. I got out the jackknife I had in my pocket and for the next hour or so we labored to get the hide off the monster. When we finished I was exhausted. Varna rolled the tiger skin into a bundle tied with rawhide straps for me to carry. She picked up the small antelope we had been carrying when we were attacked and told me with signs that there was a place to rest a short way down the trail. We left the raw carcass of the sabre tooth lying in the trail behind us. I suppose the jungle scavengers stripped the meat off the skeleton as soon as we were gone.

A mile or so farther on, Varna turned off the trail and led me up a steep hillside to a place where precipitous rock cliffs made a narrow corridor. The camp spot had evidently been used by her people before, for there were the ashes of old camp fires and the dried bones of some hunters' meal were scattered about. My lady friend gathered wood and grass for a fire and I lit it with a match. That startled her! She investigated the matchbook very carefully and I showed her how to use it. I had two books of matches, both partially used, in my pockets. I wondered how long they would last, or indeed, how long I would last in a world of cave men and sabretooth tigers.

Varna cooked me a bit of antelope meat over the fire and then spread out the raw tiger skin on the rocky ground and motioned to me that she would keep watch while I slept. The blazing noonday sun was still shining directly down on me, but I fell asleep almost immediately. My last memory was of Varna pulling thorn bushes around the entrance to the narrow canyon to block it to any large beast.

When I woke it seemed days later. Varna smiled happily to see me sit up and stretch my aching muscles. She had somehow downed a bird rather like a quail and was roasting it on a spit over the fire. Firewood had been gathered and neatly stacked between the rocks beside the fire. Varna had pulled back her long black hair and bound it with thongs of tiger hide. Her stone knife now hung in a rawhide loop at her waist. It looked as if I had been asleep for many hours, but there was no way to tell, the sun still hung at zenith, directly overhead.

As we ate, I questioned her as best I could about when the sun would set, but she shook her pretty head uncomprehendingly. Indeed, I think the natives of Pellucidar are totally lacking a sense of time. They are aware of growth and age but these things happen gradually and provide no time scale of any real utility. There is no concept of death from old age among Varna's people, but this is because in their fierce environment death always comes in the form of savage beasts or savage men.

When we had finished our second meal, the girl lay down beside me where I sat, still on the tiger hide, trustingly placed her head in my lap and fell instantly to sleep. How many hours I sat there I can not guess, not wanting to move for fear of waking her, softly stroking her long black hair where it billowed across my chest. I dared not sleep, for occasionally from the jungle below would come a harsh scream or a coughing roar as the fierce denizens of this world went about their business. I paid little attention, though, and it is well that no tiger or lion or one of the huge cave bears came to investigate our little compound, for I was lost in rosy daydreams as I sat gazing on the sleeping face of my beloved cave girl.

It was with a sense of sadness that I left that little vale in the rocks, but Varna was now anxious to push on to reach her own tribe. We were rested and fed and the bonds of affection that had linked us seemed now, to me at least, unbreakably forged.

We paused in the forest to make new bamboo spears. This time, having some idea of what we might encounter in this savage land, I chose husky poles more than two inches across and sharpened them with infinite care. We presented a strange and ferocious aspect as we continued our journey. My beard had grown a thick blond stubble over my face. I was bare-chested and now tanned by the perpetual sun. My axe hung at my belt, the last of our meat was rolled in the tiger skin and hung at my back by hide straps. I carried two eight-foot bamboo lances in one hand. My companion was still clad in the USC sweatshirt, bound around her waist now by a girdle of tigerhide. The sacrificial stone knife of the Had-bar hung at her hip and she carried three light-weight bamboo javelins with which she could bring down small game twenty paces away with deadly accuracy.

We quickly came out of the jungle into open veldt dotted with clumps of dark green trees and alive with herds of game. It looked like pictures I had seen of the plains of Africa, but nowhere in Africa or the known world were there animals such as swarmed the lush grasslands of Pellucidar. There were huge bison-like herds with wide-horned temperamental bulls. Little two and three-toed animals no bigger than dogs avoided us warily. Varna assured me they were good eating and I recognized them as the primitive ancestors of the horse. There were also herds of antelope-like animals with curving horns and of diminutive camels. Huge rhinoceros-like beasts with thick gray hides and wildly improbable sets of multiple horns on their heads roamed the plains. In the thick grasses of a lower, marshy area we came upon a score of gigantic shaggy sloths, each as big as an elephant, clumsily tearing up the ground with their huge curved claws.

Varna insisted on crossing these plains in a zigzag course so that we moved always from one clump of trees to the next, even though this doubled the distance we had to travel. I assumed that this was a precaution against lions or other predators, for the great grazing herds offered us no harm. And indeed there were lions in the veldt, we saw their tracks and heard them roaring to scatter the herds, but only once did we see a great yellow beast with a black mane moving at a distance in the grass. We hid in the brush for an hour— there were no trees nearby at the moment, but fortunately he was stalking other game and passed us by.

There were other dangers on the plains, however, that Varna had not yet warned me of, and it was for this reason that she kept always as close as possible to the trees. My first warning of this new threat was an awareness that the game herds around us were scattering wildly. Varna glanced upward and cried out, "Under the trees, quickly! Thipdar!" Fortunately, we had faithfully been pursuing her strategy of working our way from one clump of trees to another and so we were close to shelter. I followed the fleet heels of my companion until we were under the branches of a giant thorn tree and then turned to look back across the plain. As I did so there descended out of the sky, with great ungainly flapping of dragon wings, the most incredible creature I had yet seen in this incredible world. It was undoubtedly a pterodactyl, I could see the taloned fingers at the bend of each giant wing, but the size of the thing was unbelievable. Its wing span must have been 20 feet and the huge reptilian head, with its beaklike snout armed with multiple rows of teeth, was at least six feet long. The monster seized a tapir-like beast bigger than a man in its powerful rear claws and regained the air with much flapping of its hideous wings. I stood staring in amazement. Somehow, I had begun to accept the prehistoric fauna of this world as normal, but this gigantic dragon was something out of a nightmare.

"Thipdar," said Varna, "they live in the high mountains but they often seek their prey in the great herds. The only real protection from them is to get under thick trees. Then they can't come at you, for they are clumsy on the ground."

I shook my head. "We once had such things in my world," I said, "but I don't think they ever reached such size." I gazed after the slowly flying monster. The beast in its talons was still struggling weakly.

"The giant thipdars make their nests high in the mountains," Varna continued her natural history lesson. As you can see, I had progressed greatly in my ability to understand her language, although I'm taking certain liberties with her speech in translating it into English. "The Mahars are smaller but more dangerous. They capture men and women and keep them in their nests deep in the ground." This was the first I had heard of the Mahars, and strange as Varna's description was, I did not realize that she was talking about an intelligent race.

We waited a while under the trees to be sure there were no more thipdars hovering overhead waiting to swoop down upon us as soon as we left shelter. We had already slept three times and eaten twice since we began our trek across the great grassy plains. I had discovered that it was possible for me to sleep in the crotch of a tree without falling, although I still took the precaution of tying myself in with vines or rawhide straps. This always amused Varna, who could sleep lying along a tree limb, holding on with both hands and not slip off. It appeared to be a survival instinct lost to those of us on the outer surface, but extremely useful to the primitives of Pellucidar. The abundance of lions and packs of wolf-like wild dogs made such habits a necessity.

A few more "sleeps" interspersed with forced marches brought us to the edge of the great plains where low hills rose before us leading upward to green mountains tipped with snow, and Varna declared that we had entered the hunting grounds of her people. Looking back over the plains with their incredible profusion of prehistoric life, I could see the blue of the ocean behind us, as the horizonless landscape of Pellucidar literally tipped up into the air until the distance vanished into the haze. Varna assured me that the world was round with the sun in the exact center, and all my senses argued that she was right, although the whole concept of a hollow earth and its inner world seemed unbelievable.

The hills we now approached were wooded, but the vegetation was less tropical than that near the sea coast. I recognized oak, elm, beech, and several varieties of pine. Varna skirted the outskirts of the hills for several miles seeking a hidden trail which she said led to the caves of her people. Finally, she recognized a clump of tall redwoods. With a cry of delight, she led me hastily through a narrow valley and over a narrow path that led up into the hills. It was near here, she told me, that she had been captured by the Had-bar. She had been alone at the time and a party of twelve of them had run her down before she could lose them in the forest. The other two prisoners, she said, had come from another tribe.

"Are all the people who live in your world much the same?" I asked.

"All the tribes near here," she answered. "The

Mahars are different, but they are not really people. The Sagoths who serve the Mahars are like men but bigger and more hairy. They are supposed to speak to the Mahars. Far away," she gestured beyond the mountains, "there are said to be men who use great knives of metal like the little one you carry, who live in stone houses not in caves, but none of my people have ever seen them."

We proceeded along the forest trail with great care. At the foot of a great tree Varna pointed upward and I saw a deadfall of sharpened logs suspended twenty feet above my head. The girl carefully examined the ground in front of us and located the concealed rawhide thong that triggered the trap. We carefully circumnavigated the tree and its deadly burden. Half a mile further on Varna stopped again and probed the ground in front of her with her spear. She outlined for me the edge of a covered pit. "I knew where all the man-traps were when I left Val-an," she said, "but they may have put up new ones since then." At this moment we were interrupted by a long shrill bird-like whistle from the woods ahead. Varna whistled in return and a moment later we were surrounded by warriors of the Val-an tribe, laughing and calling out happily at finding the girl unharmed. They were a tall, handsome race as contrasted with the Had-bar people. Most of the men were dark, although there were a few blond beards in evidence, but none as pale as my own. Their hair was neatly trimmed or braided and their bearded faces and bodies clean except for some decorative paint in bright colors. All wore furry pelts around their loins and some wore the skins of lions as capes over their shoulders. There were necklaces and bracelets heavily in evidence, some made of teeth or claws, but many of shells or colored pebbles. They were armed with flint tipped spears or stone axes, and stone knives hung at every hip. It was a ferocious looking crowd, but their evident joy at seeing my companion prevented me from feeling any alarm. It occurred to me for the first time, however, that I might not be entirely welcome by the tribe. I withdrew slightly and stood watching, leaning nonchalantly on my spear, trying to look friendly but self-confident.

From the forest meeting we were conducted a half mile up the trail to the caves. Or rather Varna was conducted and I more or less tagged along. There was a wide open space before the sandstone cliff in which the caves were located—the tribe kept the vegetation burned off so that enemies and wild beasts could not creep up to the cave entrances. The caves themselves were truly remarkable. Originally, there must have been one large cavern through which a small stream of water ran. The stream was still there, coursing across the bare ground in front of the cliff and then down the wooded valley behind us. But now it fell twenty feet as a beautiful little waterfall. The entire entrance of the original cave had been filled in by the tribe, damming the stream and creating a clear pool inside the cave where they washed and swam. The rock for this project had been cut, by stone tools, no less, from the cliffside, creating a wide ledge twenty feet up the towering cliff and a series of artificial openings into the cave beyond. As a result, the cavern itself, a beautiful chamber of watersculpted rock and stalagtites, was illuminated by a series of artificial windows in the rock, through which the perpetual sun always shone. Access to the ledge outside was by way of a series of wooden ladders which could be hauled up for defense. We ascended these and were greeted by a crowd of more men, women, children and several ferocious looking dogs. All of these, including the dogs, fell upon Varna with cries of delight. Inside the cave had been carved by the Val-an tribe into a series of tiers or ledges rising from the central pool. The more beautiful stalagtites and stalagmites had been carefully preserved and sometimes sculpted by the primitive artists into imaginative animal and human forms. Each family unit was assigned an "apartment" on one of these levels, separated from adjacent units by natural or artificial rock formations. Overhead, the original roof of the chamber loomed a hundred feet into darkness accentuated by the smoke of the many cooking fires. At the edge of the pool was a large smooth area around a huge central fire which served as a common kitchen and town hall. Here the celebration of Varna's homecoming reached its climax, with a large number of the young people enveloping her in a mass embrace which ended in the entire group—some twenty in all—rolling on the stone floor of the cave, shrieking with laughter, surrounded by hysterically barking dogs. I sat on the side lines watching with some astonishment. I later discovered that this exuberant behavior was more or less typical of the tribe, although Varna was particularly beloved by all because of her sunny disposition and her physical beauty.

Actually, I was not being ignored. A group of curious children gathered around me, eyeing me silently until I spoke to them in their own language, which startled them very much. They broke into happy smiles and one older boy began asking me questions, but at this moment Varna extricated herself from the crowd of her admirers and came over to me. She had doffed the sweatshirt I had given her and several of the other girls were trying it on with great amusement. She was draped with necklaces of shells and colored stones which some of the young people had given her but was otherwise stark naked.

She stood next to me where I sat cross-legged on the cave floor, my tiger skin pack and my weapons beside me, and placed one hand on my shoulder and then drew up one pretty little foot and put it on the knee of her other leg so that she stood on one foot, gesticulating with her free hand. The cave people hushed and Varna began telling the tale of her adventures. Like many peoples with no written literature, story telling is an art in Varna's tribe, and she was a master of it. Her voice took on a chanting, almost sing-song quality and her tribe grouped around her, bringing up animal skins and making themselves comfortable to listen, old warriors and young children, even babes in arms, some nursing contentedly at their mother's breast.

"Oh attend and listen, tribe of Val-an," the girl began, "and I will tell you the strange and wonderful tale of my capture by the hairy horrible warriors of Had-bar. I will tell you of my imprisonment in the great cave of their tribe in the Mountains of the Clouds. I will tell you of the other prisoners of that evil people and of their terrible death on the altar of their strange glowing-eyed god. I will tell you of the miraculous appearance of Red Axe in the middle of that horde of enemies and of how he slew the priest of their god with a single blow and rescued me from sacrifice. I will tell you how the gods themselves aided us in our escape. How Red Axe led me out of the cave, killing Had-bar warriors right and left with every blow of his hand."

I started to protest this obvious exaggeration, but Varna firmly pushed me back down with her hand and I kept my mouth shut. It was worth listening to, and the tribe hung on her every word. She made much of my battle with the cave dwellers, my strange origin in another world with a different sun, and grossly exaggerated my exploits in the killing of the sabre-tooth tiger. By the time she was through she had made me out to be a hero of almost mythical proportions.

The tribe listened intently to the entire recital, and greeted the ending with wild cheering, during which Varna was again seized by the group and hugged and kissed by everybody, only this time she dragged me into the melee, which finally ended in most of us falling or being thrown into the pool. The water was invigorating but icy cold! When I tried to climb out, however, I was rushed by a bevy of nude prehistoric maidens, all shrieking with glee, and dunked again. Finally, we all gathered around the fire to dry and feast off haunches of roast wild horse. The party ended somewhat more sedately with group singing around the fire, accompanied by several of the men on stone drums—blocks of the lining stone of the cave carved into bizarre shapes, hollowed out and covered with skin or gut drum heads. I distinguished myself by teaching them "Michael Row the Boat Ashore," "On Top of Old Smokey," and other favorites from my boyhood days at summer camp. Finally, Varna led me up the tiers of stone to one of the sleeping compartments toward the back of the cave. There, in the semi-darkness, we spread a huge bear skin on the smooth stone flooring and finally fell asleep in each other's arms. My rescued maiden was home at last.

I do not know how long I stayed with Varna's people. It was always high noon when I was there. We ate, slept, sang and made love. We fished in the forest streams and I went on hunting parties with the other males. I managed to make a pretty good cave man without disgracing myself. I was poor with the javelin, but I taught them to make bows and arrows. They were faster than I and, of course, better trackers and woodsmen, but I was stronger than any and could beat them at games of strength around the camp fire. Sometimes I went berry picking with some of the girls, carrying their bark baskets for them. Usually, though, I stayed close to my darling Varna, unless I was away hunting.

"Dear," I said, one "day" as we sat beside the stream that issued from the cave and ran off through the forest, "some time I must return to the cave of the Had-bar."

"I know," she replied, laying her pretty dark head on my shoulder. She touched my bare chest with her fingertips. I had long ago had to abandon my blue jeans for the cave man's loin cloth of furry hide. I wore lizard skin sandals on my feet and carried my axe and knife in a belt of tiger skin. Otherwise, I was as bare as my lady, who today was dressed in a brief sheath of deer skin, moccasins and a string of beads around her neck.

"My own people will be trying to reach me," I said. How I was to reach the matter transmitter when it was located in the farthest recesses of a cavern occupied by an entire tribe of hostile warriors was beyond me. At this moment, however, we were interrupted by a whistle from one of the tribe's lookouts farther out in the forest.

"What's that?" I asked.

"They have a stranger," interpreted Varna. "This is very surprising. You are the first stranger who is not an enemy to enter the hunting grounds of my tribe in the memory of the oldest man. Sometimes a man comes from another tribe to steal a mate. If we catch him, we do not kill him—we beat him and send him home in disgrace." She laughed. "And the last time that happened one of our girls stole away and followed him anyway, for he was very good looking!"

I was interested in learning more the mating habits of Pellucidar, but a series of signals from the woods brought us to our feet. A party of cave men appeared in the trail, bringing with them two strangers, whom they obviously regarded with deep suspicion.

One of the party caught sight of me as Varna and I stood up to stare at the newcomers. "Red Axe!" he called, "here are two smelly Had-bar who claim to bear tokens and a message from their gods for you!"

I was unable to believe my ears. We walked slowly up to the group and stared at the newcomers. They were worth staring at. The guards had disarmed them of their spears. They were dirty, hairy, barefoot and obviously Had-bar. In addition to their animal pelt loin cloths, however, each of them wore a canvas cartridge belt, attached to which was a bayonet knife, a canvas pouch and a canteen. Each wore, on the top of his head, an old World War II metal helmet, the chin strap firmly fastened somewhere in the depths of his beard!

I burst out laughing. "Greetings, oh brothers," I said, adding in English, "but you're early for the Veterans Day Parade!"

One of the Had-bar drew himself up with great dignity. "Are you truly Red Axe, the chosen of the gods?" he asked.

"Surely, I am," I replied, trying to be as serious as he, but unable to keep from smiling.

"Then you will be able to answer this question correctly, since the gods say only the true son of their world would know the real answer," he paused for effect. I wondered what code word Doc and Tiny might have given him. I was hardly prepared for what came next.

"Knock, knock," said the cave man gravely.

I stared at him, grotesque in his helmet and fur pants, and then answered slowly, "Who's there?"

"Tiny," replied the troglodyte.

"Tiny, who," I said, though, of course, I already knew.

"Tiny Kingsly," he completed the formula, which had been conducted entirely in English. "It is indeed you, although I recognize you. I was in the temple of the gods when you first appeared." He paused and then added, "I am one of those who trapped the woman." He pointed a finger at Varna. A murmur ran through the group around us. What a dumb thing to say, I thought, he's just asking for somebody to run a spear through him. The Had-bar were not noted for their tact.

"Have you come to conduct me back to the cave of the gods?" I asked.

"Yes," replied the weirdly clad cave man. "We promised to find you in return for the weapons and things they have given us, although I don't know what use they can have for one such as you, when they have the whole Had-bar tribe to serve them. Perhaps they intend you to replace the sacrifice who escaped." He glanced around, still arrogant as all hell. "Now we will eat and rest," he announced. "We have come a long way."

"You are brave to have come so far," I conceded grudgingly, for his attitude toward Varna and her people irritated me. "Tell me your name."

"I am Gash the Mighty," he announced proudly, "and he," pointing to his companion, "is Hooka the Swift. A third of our party, Maka the Brave, was carried off by thipdars crossing the great plains. We are hungry."

I turned to the warriors around us. We stood at the edge of the bare ground in front of the entrance to the tribal cave and its waterfall. "I am sorry to admit it," I said, "but they obviously do come from my friends and I would like to have them treated well. Is it possible?"

There was an impromptu conference among the members of the tribe present. It was finally decided, as a favor to me, to bring food from the cave for the unwelcome guests, who were variously referred to as "woman-stealers" and "child-murderers" among less pleasant things. When this was done, most of us withdrew and left them alone.

"I don't like this at all," said Varna. "I do not trust them. I remember this Gash. It is lucky he comes with a message for you, or I would personally cut his throat."

"I don't like it either," I conceded, "but my friends can not help working with them as they can not move from the cave and came upon it by accident. I will go and talk to them and come right back to you."

"I wish I could feel sure of that," she said. I took her in my arms and kissed her. "Don't worry, pretty one," I whispered, "nothing can happen."

If I had only known then how devious the mind of Gash the Mighty could be.

V

PRISONERS OF THE MAHARS

A party of Val-an conducted us out of the forest to the open plains. I said a lingering farewell to

Varna under the great trees. "Be careful. Chris," she whispered, "I still do not trust them. I still think I should go with you as your fighting companion." (She used a Pellucidarian word which does not translate easily into English, it means literally "one who walks close by to guard your back.")

"I know, my dear," I whispered into her hair, "but we have talked this over. I will not have you risk capture by these people. I came all the way from my world to save you from them once—I'm not going to deliver you into their hands again."

She nodded her head against my chest obediently and then turned her face up to kiss me good-by. At the time I did not know how headstrong were the girls of the Val-an tribe. I started out on the long trek across the grasslands with their teaming herds. My two helmeted companions were not very talkative. We proceeded cautiously, always aware of the possibility of attack by the great carnivora or the flying reptiles. We each carried flint tipped spears, and the two cave men had their bayonets while I had slung my fire axe on one hip and a long stone knife on the other. I had chosen to wear my blue jeans which I had cut off above the knee. My moccasins had long since worn out and Varna had made me a pair of leather sandals from pieces of mammoth hide. In my pockets I carried my jackknife, a loop of leather thong, a spare flint spearhead, and my last few matches.

Gash led the way and I followed, Hooka behind. I felt suspiciously like a prisoner, but since they allowed me to keep my weapons, I did not complain. We followed the winding game trails from one clump of trees to another for many miles before stopping to eat. The two Had-bar brought down a large bird rather like a turkey. I wanted to build a fire and cook it. Gash was horrified.

"Do you want to signal to all our enemies with your smoke, you fool?" he snarled. "Eat it cold, or not at all!" I was forced to obey. I did not relish the raw meat but I was too hungry not to eat. I wondered how many parasites and bacteria I˙ was ingesting. It didn't improve my appetite.

Gash kept staring back down the trail behind us. Both of the cave men seemed unduly nervous, but I couldn't figure out what was bothering them.

We went on this way for two "sleeps" under the perpetual noon-day sun and several more meals. Gash insisted that we sleep in shifts, so that one of us was always awake, even when we were perched high in the trees. He was obsessed with the idea that something was tracking us. He made Hooka and I wait while he crept back down our trail on numerous occasions, but he did not find anything.

We had been traveling for what would have been days on the outer crust and had been without water for some time when we came upon a herd of sloths. These gigantic creatures were eight or nine feet high on all fours and twice that when they reared up on their hind legs to look about. They had shaggy brown coats and forepaws like shovels armed with gigantic claws. Ordinarily, we would have passed them by, they were vegetarian by habit, but they had occupied the marshy ground around the only waterhole in the area. We approached slowly and cautiously. The big creatures could be heard grunting and belching in the thick grass beside the trail. A female and several babies the size of full grown bears were wallowing like hogs in the mud at the edge of the pool. We had gotten fairly far into the tall marsh grass when there was an outburst of grunts behind us. I whirled about to see a huge bull sloth occupying the trail behind, peering at us near-sightedly and sniffing the wind.

"If he charges," whispered Gash, "run off the trail into the grass where he can't see, but keep going. They have keen noses." I was glad he had not decided to stay and fight. The big bull must have weighed two thousand pounds, and I could not imagine stopping him with a wooden spear. We stood still while the beast pawed great chunks out of the wet earth with his paws, turning his head from side to side, considering us. Perhaps he would have decided we were harmless, but at this moment one of the young pups in the water came out with a squeal and rushed us on the other side. The big bull gave a throaty roar and charged. I leaped into the reeds and mud as he went past and I heard Gash cry out in fear or pain. Hooka had disappeared into the brush on the other side of the trail, but poor Gash had turned toward the water and run head-on into the young one. They went down in a heap. The pup was squealing, Gash was hollering and the big papa was roaring as he stood over them. Fortunately, the big male was afraid to strike for fear of hitting his progeny. One sweep of those mighty paws would have cut the man in half.

Gash was clever enough to hold onto the fur of the baby sloth and try to roll both of them away from the bull. The little one, however, was clawing at the man, and it was obvious that he couldn't last long. I jumped back into the path where I was confronted by a gigantic hairy rump. I gave the old boy a sharp jab with my spear where it would do the most good. He let out a grunt of surprise and sat down on his haunches and turned toward me.

"Come on, you big lug!" I yelled, dancing in front of him. "Nyah, nyah, nyah, can't catch me!"

He took the bait—or tried to—and came after me. I turned tail and ran. The ground behind me shook as the sloth started in pursuit. I was running easily, sure I could outdistance the clumsy beast until I heard his breathing behind me. I glanced over my shoulder. Clumsy or not, he was coming along like an express train. I came out of the tall grass onto the green open plain with a fresh burst of speed. The nearest clump of trees was two hundred yards away. I started for it at my best backfield run. After me came two tons of enraged beefsteak.

I figured if I could get among the trees I could dodge my pursuer long enough to climb a tree and be out of reach. When we reached the trees, however, he was close on my heels. I wheeled around a tall oak and started scrambling up the branches on the far side. The sloth reared up to his full height and grabbed the branch I was on and began tearing it off the tree trunk. His claws were hooked onto the branch of either side of me. I had dropped my spear. Clinging to the swaying branch with one arm I pulled my axe out of its belt loop with the other hand. The tree limb began to tear loose. Something flashed past my head. Hanging now by one hand I looked down at the giant sloth as he gave a squeal of pain. To my amazement I saw the shaft of a javelin protruding out of one of his little pig-like eyes. He fell back, clawing at his face with his great paws. I leaped up to the next branch, and turned to confront my rescuer. Her black hair fell about her in disarray, her eyes flashed, and she clung to a tangle of vines behind her, a second spear still ready in one hand.

"Are you alright?"

"Yes, thanks to you."

She lowered her spear and I my axe. I stepped out on the branch and caught her in my arms. As the giant sloth roared his pain and frustration below us we stood, thirty feet above the ground, lost in a long and lingering kiss.

"You had no business following me alone like that," I said, some time later, "you might have gotten killed."

Varna laughed happily. "Who was about to be killed when I arrived?" she asked. There was no arguing that. A long time later the sloth went away and the two Had-bar appeared at the foot of the tree. Gash escaped unharmed except for a few scratches on his skin and his pride.

"Come on down, Red Axe," he called, "we know you are still hiding up there. The dryath is gone, I have frightened it away."

"Frightened it away, hell," I replied, "if I hadn't stabbed it in the rear there would be nothing left of you but a grease spot."

"For the son of a god, you run well," grinned Gash the Mighty. He did have a point there. "I see the woman has shown up. I knew someone was tracking us."

"If Red Axe did not run well he would not be here to receive the thanks of his friend Gash whose life he just saved," I replied. The sarcasm of this was lost on the cave man. "Yes, the girl will join us for the rest of the trip." I had already tried to persuade Varna to return to her people. She refused point-blank and since I did not feel like carrying her back over my shoulders that was that.

"Of course," said the Had-bar, "she must join us. It would not be safe for her to travel the wild country alone."

"On the contrary," I said, "it would not be safe for me." He only grunted.

When we stopped to sleep, Gash chose a dense thorn thicket where he said it would be safe for us to sleep on the ground. I had the first watch and then woke Hooka and stretched out beside Varna. I was awakened sometime later by her scream. I tried to spring up and found myself restrained by a loop of rawhide rope around my arms and torso. The two Had-bar fell on me and tied my hands together behind my back. Gash confronted me as they pulled me erect. Varna was already similarly bound.

"You ungrateful bastard," I snarled, "just see if I ever save your life again!"

"You are unlikely to have the chance, where you are going," he replied with a wicked grin. "Now, move!" and he prodded me with his spear.

They forced us both to walk out of the brush onto the plain. We followed the trail we had been on. The two Had-bar did not indulge in much conversation, so Varna and I talked to each other.

"I am sorry now that I did not tell you," she remarked, "they have not been heading back toward the Had-bar caves. They turned aside a day ago. I wondered if you had not noticed."

"No," I replied, "I do not know these trails. I knew we were not on the path you brought me."

She seemed surprised at this. Questioning her, I discovered that the natives of Pellucidar have a homing instinct or directional sense. They can find their way to any place they have been—without, of course, any help from the sun or the stars. How they did this Varna could not tell me. She was amazed that I could not simply "know" in which direction Val-an lay, or the caves of the Had-bar.

"Perhaps there is something wrong with you, Christopher," she suggested. "Were you ever hit on the head as a baby?"

"Perhaps," I said, "but I don't think so. Where do you think they are taking us?"

"I can't figure it out," she replied, "we are headed out into the plains, away from the hunting grounds of any tribe I know." She paused and then added, in a hushed voice, almost to herself, "Except the Mahars."

"Hey, Gash," I called, "where are you taking us?"

The Had-bar grunted. We had been walking at a brisk pace and the sweat glistened on his hairy face under his grotesque helmet. "You'll find out soon enough," he grinned.

"What will you tell the great gods in the back of the cave?" I inquired.

"That you were killed and eaten by lions," he answered ingeniously. "It is too bad that the woman has to know the truth, for I would like to take her back with me as my mate."

"I would sooner mate with a silith," hissed Varna.

"Shut up," the cave man cried, striking her with the shaft of his spear.

"You are going to be sorry you did that, Gash," I remarked, "if I ever get my hands free."

"You shut up, too," he yelled, hitting me with the butt end of his spear across the back, "shut up both of you."

After that we walked a long way in silence. Fortunately, we were not attacked by any of the large carnivores. I could have offered little defense with my hands tied behind my back, and the heroic Had-bar would have undoubtedly run off and left both of us to our fate. Gash did not know I had my knife in my pocket, and I hoped during the next sleep to get it out and cut our bonds. This plan was frustrated by the next series of events, however.

Gash led us to the top of a low rise covered with thorn bush. Going to a thicket of this he began pulling off the branches and soon to my amazement, uncovered an iron cage, six feet high and three feet wide, the bars being about four inches apart.

"Mahars!" breathed Varna. Looking at her, I saw that her face was white with fear.

"What does it mean, Varna?" I asked.

"Mahars," she repeated, "only the Mahars make such things. They are going to give us to the Mahars."

I couldn't understand why she was so alarmed. To me, the iron cage—Gash was now struggling to get the door open while Hooka watched us suspiciously—to me the cage spelled civilization. Civilization of some sort, I reflected, although that did not mean an improvement in our lot. I still had no inkling of the nature of the dominant race of Pellucidar.

Gash forced us both into the cage and fastened the door shut. The latch seemed simple enough, but he locked it from the outside. Varna and I crowded together, our hands still tied. The cage was too small for us to do anything but stand, pressed together. Varna leaned against me, her face against my chest. The two Had-bar went a short distance away and began a fire. They were still in sight, and I did not dare try my escape plan yet.

When they got the fire going the cave men put handfuls of green grass on it until it began to smoke. It was a quiet "day" and the column of white smoke rose almost straight up into the bright blue sky. They kept the smoke signal going for about half an hour and then let it die out. They came back and squatted on the ground near the cage, waiting for something. I was waiting, too, with great curiosity.

Two specks appeared in the sky. Hooka pointed. Gash rose to his feet, shading his eyes with his hand, watching. The distance dots grew as they drew near until I could see that they were gigantic pterodactyls. To my surprise, the Had-bar did not run for cover, but stood calmly watching them. They circled the hilltop several times and I saw that perched on their necks were human riders. Gash waved his arm in greeting and the two huge flying lizards swooped low and made a clumsy landing in the grass nearby. Their riders sprang to the ground and I could now see that they held some sort of reins attached to the monsters' necks. These they fastened to the ground before advancing towards us.

The two thipdar riders were as remarkable as their mounts. As they approached, I saw that, although thy walked fully erect, they were more like gorillas than men. Their faces and bodies were completely covered with short black hair. They wore leather vests and a sort of kilt over their loins. They were armed with long knives in leather sheaths and huge wooden cudgels. Their wrinkled, flat nosed faces and dark little eyes made them look fierce. One of them spoke, and his voice was clear and deep. He spoke the common language of the cave people and Varna and I could understand him perfectly.

"Ho, gilak," he greeted Gash with almost contempt, "have you captured the one our masters want? Who is this female?"

"She is his mate," Gash replied, "we had to take both of them together."

"It is good," said the man-ape, "the masters may wish to breed them. Here is the reward we promised." He held a skin wrapped parcel up for Gash to see. The Had-bar stepped forward and took it, but as he did so the gorilla man seized him by the throat in one huge hand and lifted him off the ground. At that very instant the other man-ape hurled his club with deadly accuracy, striking Hooka on the forehead and laying him out on the ground senseless, perhaps dead. Gash struggled mightily but he was no match for his antagonist, who stood over six feet tall and was muscled like the ape he resembled. The gorilla man waited until the Had-bar went limp, then opened the cage door and pushed him in with the two of us. The Had-bar was blue, but he was starting to breathe again.

The man-ape carefully fastened the cage door, ignoring the two of us, and spoke to his companion who turned, leaving poor Hooka on the ground and returned to the giant thipdars. He remounted one of the beasts and they took to the air. I thought for a moment that he had gone for reinforcements, but then I saw the flying reptile turn and swoop towards us. The next instant its talons had seized the top of the cage. With a crash and a violent jerk, it lifted us up off the ground. Varna and I gasped with amazement as the ground fell away beneath us. I could see the second gorilla-man run for his mount and soon the two were flying through the savage sky side by side. The cage did not swing, for the pterodactyl had a firm grip on the top bars, but it was held at an angle and the rush of trees, meadow and grazing herds below us was dizzying. Varna crouched against me, whimpering with fright. Gash had slumped against one corner of the cage, but he gradually regained consciousness, and, when he did, he gave a moan of terror and clutched the bars with both hands, watching the world wheel beneath us.

I think that wild ride through the air was the most terrifying thing that happened to me in all my adventures in Pellucidar. I tried telling myself that the giant pterodactyl was accustomed to carrying its prey in its talons and that there was no likelihood of our being dropped. The dizzying sweep of field and jungle below us was, however, far from reassuring. I found it easier to take with my eyes shut, holding the side of the cage with my hands tied behind my back, Varna's face hidden against my chest.

"Varna," I whispered to her, "turn and put your hand in my pocket, find the knife."

"Oh, Chris, what if I drop it? We'll lose it!"

"We'll have to take the chance. I need my hands free if we are ever to escape."

"No one escapes," she replied. "No one ever escapes from the Mahars."

"Get the knife," I said. The only answer to the conviction of impending defeat is to take positive and aggressive action. But when Varna's little fingers located the jackknife in my pocket her wrists had been bound for some time and her grip was weak. She got the knife out but could not open it. Struggling in the narrow cage I turned my back to her and took the knife in nerveless fingers. My touch was numb and with difficulty I identified the groove on the cutting blade and got my thumb nail into it. Slowly I pulled, trying to maintain a firm hold on the handle without impeding the opening of the blade. The flying monster made a lurch in the air, throwing me against the iron bars. The knife fell from my grip with a clink on the floor of the cage.

Looking down I saw it balanced precariously on a cross bar. Thousands of feet below sped the lush greenery of a jungle, tropic birds whirling above the branches. The open knife teetered on its rest. In a moment it would plunge through the space between the bars and be lost forever. I started to slide into a slow squat, hoping against hope to get my hands into position to grab it. A huge hairy foot seemed to appear from nowhere and plop down

71

upon the knife handle. Startled, I looked up. Grinning at me across the cage was Gash, the jackknife clutched in one prehensile foot.

"Now, Red Axe," he grinned, "what is it worth to you to have your bonds cut?"

"Gash," I said, "much as I hate to admit it, you still have the upper hand, or, in this case, the upper foot." Gash quickly transferred my jackknife to his left hand, holding firmly to the bars of the flying cage with his right. He seemed ready to stick it into my ribs. I braced myself to block him if he came towards us.

"Look Christopher," cried Varna, "below us, the city of the Mahars!"

Gash and I both turned to gaze downward. Our pterodactyl was rapidly descending toward a wide clearing in the jungle. Twenty massive stone towers encircled an open grassy plain in which I could see a number of shafts or tunnels into the earth. The tops of the towers were manned with armed Sagoths, as the gorilla men are called, many of whom pointed and waved to us as our winged monster began to circle and descend. Small flying reptiles glided to and fro between the towers or walked clumsily on the ground. It didn't look much like a city, but I was unaware that the Mahars build mostly underground. Indeed, I was still unaware of the nature of the Mahars—I thought Mahars were the ape-men who had taken us captive.

"Quick, Gash," I urged, "our chances of escape are greater if we work together. Free us and at the first opportunity we will all make a break for freedom. I will be of no use to you bound, but with my hands free we can work together."

"I don't trust you, Red Axe," he replied, "I will free the woman because I mean to take her with

72

me if I can escape. You I intended to give to the Mahars anyway."

"If you're going to free anyone, you'd better hurry," I cried, "because here comes the ground!" And with that the thipdar swooped low over the open plain between the towers, its great membrane wings raising a cloud of dust and leaves, leveled off and dropped the cage with a fearful clang, rolling it, and us, over and over. A crowd of human forms ran towards us as the reptiles flapped off out of sight. I ended up lying on my back on top of Gash and Varna and, wonder of wonders, I felt in my hand the cold steel of the knife. I slipped it away from Gash, who seemed stunned by the fall. "Varna, Varna, are you hurt?" I cried, as I closed the knife behind me and worked it into a hip pocket of my pants.

"No, Christopher, only bruised, I think," called the girl, "but this ugly Had-bar is crushing me with his weight."

By this time several men had reached the cage and opened the door—which was now on one side. They rolled us out in the dust and we scrambled to our feet. The gorilla men, armed with clubs or spears, which I was surprised to see had steel tips, stood back warily. The humans, for there were a number of them, were unarmed and wore only loincloths of soft hide and leather sandals. They were pale and flabby—not as healthy as the tribes of wild cave men I had met. I supposed that captivity had not been too healthy for them.

"Ho, gilaks," grunted a big ape, "stand still, we will cut your bonds." So much, I thought, for my big escape plans.

"Which one of you is the stranger from the land of the Had-bar?" said the leader of the armed party.

"He is," said my friend Gash, pointing at me. "I am Gash, of the Had-bar, who captured him and delivered him into the hands of the noble Sagoths. Having done this I now demand that I be returned to my people."

"You look like a troublemaker to me," said the Sagoth commander, "give me any back talk and I'll run you through." Turning to several of his "men" he said, "The tall blond male goes to the place of the Twelves. The ugly one and female to the pens."

"Wait," I said, "she is my mate. She goes with me."

The big brute came up to me. He was taller than I and he scowled down at me. "You another troublemaker?" he asked. "I kill you as quickly as the other."

"No," I said, "you will not. I am the one your masters sent for. You will deliver me alive. My mate goes with me. If not, I fight you all now—to the death." I drew my axe from my belt. It was a desperate gamble. For all I knew the gorilla man did not have any special orders about me. I could not, however, let Varna be taken from me without a fight. The ape-man grunted, eyeing me as if trying to judge my determination. The other humans fell back a few steps as if horrified at my defiance. Varna, brave girl, came and stood beside me—on my left so that my right arm would be free to fight.

At this moment a bizarre figure made its way through the crowd around us. It was a pterodactyl, smaller than the gigantic creature that had carried us here, and it walked erect, the long toothed beak stuck forward, the wing tips held up high over its head, its snake-like tail dragging on the ground. The men and Sagoths gave way, making room for the creature to approach us. I could see the great round eyes regard us as the beast turned its head from side to side, looking at us first with one eye, then with the other. I was surprised to note a metal medallion of some sort around its neck, and metal bracelets on each ankle above the taloned feet.

The reptile turned toward the leader of the Sagoths. He looked strangely flustered for a moment and then dropped his cudgel and began a strange performance of finger and hand movements in front of his face. I watched for a while before I noticed that the fingers of the wing tips of the flying reptile were also moving. Then I realized why the bizarre scene was familiar. It resembled two deaf people talking by sign language. Indeed, this is exactly what it was, for the reptiles are completely deaf. We watched for a moment, then the Sagoth sighed and turned to his troops. "Take them all to the Twelves," he said, "the Great One orders it."

The pterodactyl turned one bright beady eye on me again, unblinking it returned my gaze for a long moment. Somehow I got the impression that it was both curious and friendly.

"Varna," I asked, without turning my head or eyes from the creature, "what is this thing?"

Her hand touched my arm and I felt a shiver run through her. "Don't you know, Christopher?" she breathed, "it is one of the Mahars, the ones who now hold us captive."

Aghast, I watched as the reptile turned and walked away. The people around us stepped back respectfully to allow it to pass.

VI

HUMAN GUINEA PIG

The city of the Mahars was a huge underground hive. The descending ramps and open areas below were illuminated by the perpetual sunlight of Pellucidar streaming through shafts in the roof. Eight and twelve story buildings were carved out of the rock and the interior of these were illuminated by what looked like gas lights—at least a luminous flame appeared in the center of the glass globes that hung from the ceilings. We were conducted rapidly into one of the larger buildings. Gash was taken with us, much to my disgust, for I had tired of his company. If I ever saw Gash the Had-bar again, I said to myself, I hoped he would be on the wrong end of a spear. Then I realized that I was, myself, thinking like an uncivilized savage and was shocked. How quickly we revert to our primitive drives for survival when the going gets rough! I resolved to suppress my instincts more effectively in the future.

Our weapons were turned over to a big Sagoth and we were then led to a small chamber in the basement of one of the larger buildings by a man. He was tall and slender and very pale as if he rarely saw the sun. Even his hair was bleached white, although he appeared quite young.

"I am Elak," he introduced himself to us, "you three will sleep here. When the bell rings, come out and join the others in the corridor here. We all march to our meals together. It is permitted to talk quietly but not to make much noise. The Sagoths in charge here treat us pretty well, but they will not stand for noise and confusion. They say it disturbs the Great Ones, but that is nonsense, for the Great Ones are deaf. I do not know what your assignments will be, perhaps later the Sagoths will tell you, or me. Rest now, while you can."

"Wait, Elak," I said, as he turned to leave the store room. "Is it true that no one has ever escaped from a Mahar City?"

He sighed. "I knew you would have to ask that question. Every new gilak who comes here wants to escape. Do you see that there are no doors to your cave? Do you see that the Sagoths do not guard the entrance to the building? If you get out of the city you are immediately seen by the Sagoths on the guard towers and they can fill you full of spears before you can cross the plain."

I realized once again how strangely my mind works compared with the natives of Pellucidar, for my first thought was "we could make it at night." I had to stop and think before I realized that this was impossible—for there is no night in all the inner world.

Elak was continuing, "And if one got across the plain of Phuma—which is impossible, for if the Sagoths were to miss you with their spears, they can call up the giant thipdars from their lairs in the other side of the city to hunt you down—but even if you could escape into the jungle, where would you go? The jungle is full of huge meat-eating monsters. There are no other cities nearby, no food and no shelter. If the great killer lizards didn't get you, you would die of cold and hunger."

Varna, Gash and I stared at the man in amazement. "You've never been outside the city, have you?" I asked. He shook his head.

"You poor worm," scoffed Gash, "we Had-bar can

77

live anywhere in the forest. We are not afraid of the clumsy meat-eaters. When we are hungry we eat them."

Elak looked incredulous. "I was born here, as were all my people. You wild gilaks from the outside may boast of your strength and your courage, but you will never escape from the city of Phuma." He turned on his heel and left.

"You should not have made fun of him, Gash," said Varna. "He knows nothing of the outside world he has lived all his life underground."

"Yes," I agreed, "and we need all the friends we can get if we are to escape from this ant's nest. What do you think they intend to do with us?"

"Keep us here until we turn soft and white like that worm," grumbled Gash, settling himself on the stone floor, "now shut up so I can sleep." Soon the ugly cave man was snoring loudly and happily, and Varna and I, exhausted by our wild ride through the sky of Pellucidar in the talons of the giant pterodactyl, were quick to join him.

We were awakened by the ringing of a bell and herded to our meal with several dozen other humans, men, women and children. Most of them were the pale albino city people, but there was a sprinkling of dark hairy wild men, mostly dressed in their furry untanned hides. We helped ourselves to a meat stew and handfuls of raw fruits and vegetables. I sought out Elak and crouched down next to him. There were, of course, no tables or chairs in the room, which was dimly illuminated by a single shaft of sunlight.

"Elak," I said, "I am called Red Axe and this is Varna, my mate. I am sorry the Had-bar with us spoke to you as he did. He is no friend of mine, for he trapped us and turned us over to the Sagoths."

The pale man only nodded, watching my face intently with his blue eyes. "What do you want?" he asked. He was sitting with a woman of his own people who held a tiny babe to her breast. I assumed her to be his mate.

"What do the Sagoths intend to do with us?" I asked.

"You are here for purposes known only to the Mahars themselves," he replied. "Most of us work here in the building, cleaning and repairing the rooms. Some wash and clean the strange devices the Mahars use in their work. The Sagoths tell us what to do—the Mahars talk only to the Sagoths with the language of signs. The Great Ones talk to each other in some other way I do not understand. My people say they talk with their minds—one mind to another."

Telepathy! Was it possible, I wondered? The evidence for telepathy in my own world was shaky to say the least, but what might be possible to such strange creatures as the reptilian Mahars?

A big burly Sagoth, armed with a giant club, entered the room and walked his way through the crowd until he spotted me. "Ho, gilak!" he called, gesturing me over. I kissed Varna's forehead and walked over to him. Whatever the Mahars wanted of me, it seemed I was about to discover it.

I was led to the upper stories of the building, my glimpses into the rooms we passed were illuminating and surprising. They were all scientific laboratories! The apparatus was strange but I saw the reptilian Mahars working with chemical glassware, with distillation apparatus of some sort, with electrical machines powered by banks of huge batteries, and with fishes in a huge dark tank. It was strangely exciting for me to be in an environment similar to the one I had left behind on the outer world.

I had no time for further investigation, however, for my guard took me forcibly by the arm and hurried me up a ramp and into a small room. This room had a door and he shut it firmly behind me, and I discovered by pushing against it, locked it from the outside. The room was bare stone, barely high enough for me to stand erect. I searched it all over but could find no way out. There was a small hole in the center of the floor and another in the center of the ceiling, each large enough to admit my finger. Light came from one of the gas flame lamps, but this was set in the wall and shielded by a metal grill.

What on earth, I wondered, did they intend to do with me? I had the distinct impression that I was being watched although I could see nothing through the ceiling and floor holes. I waited a while in silence and then lay on the floor and, out of pure boredom, fell asleep.

I was awakened some time later by a faint noise. As I opened my eyes, I was surprised to see one wall of the room sliding up into the ceiling. In the dim light of several flame globes, I saw a long corridor facing me—narrow, no wider than three feet —but twenty to thirty feet long. Nothing loath, I walked out of my cell down the passage, arriving at a cross corridor running left and right.

What was I supposed to do now, I wondered? I stood a few moments, turning my head and eyes right and left. The two passageways looked equally bare and uninviting. Finally, I chose the left by mentally flipping a coin and having it come up heads. I crept down the corridor with some caution, for I had now a vague premonition of danger. I wanted to get out my knife, which was still in my pants pocket, but I had the definite feeling of being watched. Gilaks were supposed to have been disarmed, I decided in favor of secreting my one weapon.

The next cross corridor looked like the first, and so did the next, and the next. I was beginning to get tired of walking when I came to a dead end. The passage simply came up to a smooth stone wall. I felt over it carefully but could find no way of opening it. Discouraged, I sat down on the floor with my back to the wall and rested. I was beginning to get thirsty and even hungry. I wondered how long I had been in the empty stone hallways.

Finally, I decided that I could wait until I starved to death, or I could wander up and down again in hopes of finding a way out—or better yet, something to eat. It was many turns later that I came back to my cell—or what I took to be the cell. The passage came again to a dead end, but this time there was something on the floor. Hurrying up, I discovered to my amazement a piece of meat and a clay cup of water! I gulped down both items. They were hardly enough to take the edge off my thirst and hunger, so, after waiting a while to see if the door would open and release me, I wandered off again. I had only gone one turn when it occurred to me to take the cup with me. I turned back and retraced my steps. The cup was gone!

There could be no mistake, I could see the wet ring in the dust where I had put it down. I tried the door again, but it felt like a solid stone slab. After waiting a bit, I returned to my random wandering of the corridors. I still felt a creepy sensation that someone was watching me.

About ten turns farther on I came to another cell at the end of a passage and found another piece of meat and another cup of water. At least I wasn't going to starve immediately, although I wondered how long I could keep going on such short rations. I sat down and ate my dry meat slowly, since it seemed that I might have to walk a long way to find another.

"I wonder," I said aloud to myself, "how long I'm going to wander through this maze?"

A cold chill went down my spine. Of course, that's what it was—a maze! Exactly like the ones I used to train animals at the University labs! Why hadn't I recognized it immediately? A start box, a series of turns—I suddenly realized I had no idea how many—and a food reward at the end of the run. Someone must be counting the time and number of turns it took me to learn the thing. I had a mental image of an intelligent pterodactyl with a ball point pen and a clip board recording my every move.

Now that I knew what I was up against, I set about methodically unravelling the maze. First, I broke the cup on the floor and scratched an X on the wall and set out at a rapid walk down the passage. "Left, right, left, right," I muttered, memorizing as I went, "Oops." I'd come to a dead end. I retraced my steps and "re-did" the turn. Sure enough I eventually came to a cell with fresh meat and water. There was no mark on the wall.

"Aha!" I cried. Quickly I mapped from memory the course I had come from the other feeding room —I was already thinking of them as "reward chambers." The most efficient design, I decided, would be to have one feeding spot at one end of the maze and one at the other.

Thus, I would be forced to shuttle back and forth, and my testers would merely bait first one side and then the other. They would not have to move me back to the "start box" for each run.

I finished my snack, memorized the map and retraced my steps as quickly as possible. I made one wrong turn and soon corrected myself. I arrived, as I had expected, at a reward chamber where the wall was marked by an X scratched on the stone. I carefully drew a corrected map on the floor with my cup fragment and ate the meat and drank the water. Then I set out to back track my course to the other reward station. The food and water were there. Did I detect a swirl in the cup of water as if it had just been set down? I gulped down the water and picked up the meat, holding it in my hand I started back. If they wanted to play this game, I thought, at least I'd keep them busy.

I made what must be ten runs from one end of the maze to the other without a mistake and finally sat down at one end to rest. I was no longer hungry or thirsty, but I was tired! I had just finished eating when the slab descended from the roof, closing me in.

I had only a moment to panic, wondering if I should have tried to get out of my start box into the body of the maze. Then the back wall opened up. A big ugly Sagoth stood there. I couldn't tell if he was the same one who had brought me there. They all looked alike to me. "Come on, gilak," he grunted, "back to your home cave." I followed him willingly. My mind was a whirl of excitement. I was in the hands of an intelligent race who were using me for psychological experiments. How could I communicate with them—how could I turn this to my own advantage? Were the Mahars truly telepathic? I must find Elak and get more information.

Varna went wild with delight at the sight of me. Time had passed rapidly for me in the maze, but for her, waiting patiently, with nothing to do, it has seemed that I was gone an eternity.

"I have eaten and slept and slept and eaten,

since you were taken away," she cried, "and I had decided that you were surely dead. At the very first opportunity I intended to kill myself."

It took me a long while to soothe her fears, and then she had to hear the entire story of my adventure. When she finally fell asleep I left her and went in search of Elak.

The pale man heard me out without interruption. "I have some influence with the Sagoths, Red Axe," he said finally, "but none at all with the Mahars themselves. Do you really think there would be some advantage to your talking to them?"

"I think there would be," I said with great conviction, "particularly those who were working with me today. Perhaps I can get them to provide better care for all of us, in exchange for things I can tell them."

Elak shook his head doubtfully, "Some of us can get through to the Sagoths," he admitted, "but we have no direct communication with the Great Ones themselves. However, I will see what can be done."

This certainly was not very satisfying. As I returned to the room assigned to Varna and myself, (I had gotten Elak to find Gash sleeping quarters elsewhere) I tried to think of other ways to get to the Mahar psychologists the fact that I was fully as intelligent as they and that they should try to enlist my voluntary cooperation. Elak apparently belonged to some sort of unofficial informer system linked to the Sagoths who, after all, had most of the direct contact with us slaves. That was worth knowing, although at that moment I did not have any real use for the information.

But I was not given an opportunity to get a message through channels before I was brought back to the psychological laboratory. I ate and slept and then the Sagoth guard came for me. I went willingly for I was anxious to communicate with the Mahar scientists.

I was shut into another small cell. There was a small hole in the wall—large enough to put my hand into—but I could find nothing. There was a light globe in a wall recess and the usual holes in the floor and ceiling. I suspected these were peekholes for the reptilian observers, but I could see nothing by looking into them. Sticking out of the wall about a foot was a short thick rod. I tried to pull or push it, but nothing happened. I sat down to wait.

This would never do, I thought. There must be a way I could get through to the probable observers that I was an intelligent being, one they should be glad to work with. Well, why didn't I do something intelligent? I looked around the room. There was the light and the rounded pole stuck out of the wall. That was all. Hard to think of anything intelligent to do, under the circumstances. If I knew the Sagoth-Mahar sign language, I could madly signal for my release, but I knew not a single word —or sign.

The light dimmed briefly, then brightened again. There was a loud click from the wall. I got up to investigate. There was something small and round in the hole in the wall. I took it out. It was a nut. Idly, I cracked it open and ate it as I stood there. The light flickered again and there was a click, and a nut fell into the aperture in the wall. I picked it up and waited. A few moments and the entire process was repeated. I still hadn't figured out what was going on.

Now the light dimmed and brightened and nothing happened. I stood looking at the hole in the wall for a while and then put my hand out behind

85

me. I touched the wooden rod in the wall—strictly by accident—and it moved. There was an immediate click! And a fourth nut appeared in the hole.

I stared at it in amazement. A "Skinner box!" I was in a giant testing box of the type Professor Skinner of Harvard had invented for the rat and the pigeon.*

Now that I knew what test I was being subjected to, I could quickly solve the problems. At least, so I thought. The first was easy—each time the light dimmed and then brightened again the lever was "activated", it was "time in" and a lever press yielded a nut. Only one lever press at a time worked, however, as I quickly discovered. I soon tired of eating the nuts, but I continued to respond with a lever press to each light signal, merely piling the nuts in a corner of the test box.

"There," I said, as I piled a dozen nuts together, "one of you can write a thesis on 'Hoarding Behavior in Homo Sapiens Terrestrialis.'"

Now the light globe was slipped out—very neatly so I couldn't see who did it, leaving me in dark-

*Editor's note: It certainly is surprising that the Mahar psychologists should use the same apparatus to test the responses of human beings that human psychologists use to test other animal species. This is not the first incidence of this, however. Dr. James McConnell has reported how certain extraterrestrial scientists performed very similar tests on a captured human psychologist. ("Learning Theory" by J. V. McConnell, in *The Worm Re-Turns*, Prentice-Hall, 1965.) It is difficult to tell what this remarkable duplication of methods in three intelligent species might mean. One is inclined to speculate that there are only very limited ways of studying learning in another species, but this seems a rather pessimistic viewpoint. Perhaps it only means that the brains of the Mahars of Pellucidar, the homo-sapiens of the outer crust, and the unknown interstellar travelers of McConnell's story are all very similar. Does this mean that we represent the ultimate in organic intelligence? I certainly hope not.

ness for five minutes or so. Then two smaller globes were inserted into my test box. One was red and the other green. That was an easy one—a few trials taught me that the red light meant that the lever was "on" and the green that it was "off". Twenty-four nuts later the lights changed to yellow and blue and I had to learn how that combination worked. Then I had a short break and a pan of water pushed in through a new hole that suddenly appeared at floor level.

I ate a few nuts and went over the situation in my mind. The reptilian psychologists were obviously testing my ability to discriminate colors. Next would be tones—no, probably not, since they were themselves rumored to be deaf. Maybe telepathy? That is how Elak said they communicated among themselves.

My immediate problem was to convince them that I could communicate with them more directly. That would be of greater advantage to them. Or would it? I had a sudden chill of apprehension. Maybe this creature was only interested in color vision. I knew scientists on the surface world who were so deep into the minutia of problems like this that if their rats had slipped them a note written in English they would have discarded it as "poor data" and "irrelevant to the problem at hand." Worse yet, they would probably "discard" the animals that didn't work with the problem. If that happened to me, I would lose my chance of communicating with the master race of Pellucidar—I might even lose my life!

With that the lights came on again. It was the red-green problem, now interspersed with the blue-yellow one. To see if I still remembered it, I suppose. Then we switched to two shades of violet. Each "set" of problems ran 24 times and then stopped. The Mahars must count by twelves, I noted to myself. What other useful conclusions could I draw about their psychology by observing how they tested me? Well, they had color vision and they were motivated by hunger.

Now what was wrong? The globes had ceased to flash. I waited patiently, tapping the lever with my fingernails. Time dragged by—I had no way of measuring it in my dark box. After what seemed an incredibly long time, the lights returned with the red-green discrimination. Then on to two shades of red. Then again a long pause. What was going on?

I pressed close to the grill which separated me from the two globes. One was warm! I waited, the warmth stopped, then a few moments later the other became warm. They were still testing me. In the infra-red!

"You're right," I remarked to the wall, "I can't see in the far red. I can't see ultra violet, which is probably what you were using in the earlier trial. I can feel the heat from your apparatus, though, you probably didn't control for that. Maybe I could discriminate two different heat levels. . . ."

I thought about trying that, holding my hands before the globes I could tell from the radiated warmth when one was on, although I could see nothing at all. Further reflection made me give up the idea of trying to guess which radiation was the "on" signal.

"Somebody is testing human-gilak vision," I said to myself, "and I've found a hole in his method. If I use it, I won't be telling him a thing—he'll just think I can see into the far red. I won't fight the problem—I'll just be a good little rat and only lever press when I'm supposed to. After all, I want to become the laboratory favorite, if I can."

On and on went the testing, and still I could

think of no way to get into direct contact with my scientist captors. When I left the test box and was returned to the living quarters I was no nearer to a solution to my problem.

"Hey, you want these nuts?" asked the big Sagoth who came to get me.

"No," I replied. "Leave them. They can use them next time."

The next few "days" were spent in testing the limits of my visual acuity. Could I tell the difference between two shades of green? Yes, I could. So then the greens were made so similar that I began making mistakes. And so with the reds, blues and yellows. Then there were differences in brightness—both lights on simultaneously, if the left is brighter than the right, press the lever, get a nut. Slowly the two are made so similar that I could not tell the difference. Twenty-four trials in which I failed and got chance scores—half right, half wrong—and then back to something else. I admired the persistence of the experimenter—until it occurred to me that I had to be at least as persistent as he. I wonder if he ever thought of that?

Meanwhile, Varna was put to work cleaning glassware on the second floor and the mighty Gash was made part of a work-party that daily carried all the trash out of the building and burned it in a pit at the end of the plain. Gash thus got to see the outdoors and the pens where the giant thipdars were kept. I told him that it was appropriate that he be made a garbage collector, but he got back at me by pointing out that I was getting as pale as Elak.

I suppose I should have been worried about getting back to the matter transmitter. Actually, I was having a rather good time in my efforts to figure out how to get through to the Mahars. I tried leaving geometrical messages scratched on the walls and floor of my test box. I put down a diagram of Pythagorean Theorum that the square of the hypotenuse is equal to the squares on the other two sides of a triangle, and I tried to indicate that the circumference of a circle was equal to pi times the radius squared, but I don't think my Mahar captors ever looked into the box when I wasn't there.

Varna hated the laboratories and the Mahars as well. She had been talking to the other women and she told me that periodically one of the slaves would vanish. "They think the Mahars eat them," she said.

"Nonsense," I replied. "The Mahars are an intelligent race. There are any number of other explanations. Perhaps they are merely transferred to another building." Little did I know!

At one of the meals, Varna and I sat next to one of the pale city people whom I had not noticed before. He seemed uncommonly interested in our conversation. As we got up to leave, he obviously gathered his nerve enough to speak to me.

"My name is Tarmash," he said, blocking my way deferentially. "I heard you telling your mate about being in the box with the colored lights. I am taken every day to a small cave and made to look at colored light globes."

"Really?" I asked, suddenly interested. "Tell me about it," but before he could begin Elak came over to us. In a very conspiratorial manner he whispered that we were to meet in his cell on the lower level as soon as we could get away. It seemed the "underground organization" of slaves had finally accepted me. Tarmash, Varna and I strolled out as nonchalantly as we could while the pale city man told me of his experiences in the laboratory.

It was obvious from what he said that the man

was another subject of the same laboratory that was working on me. I explained as best I could what the Mahar scientists were doing with us. It was difficult because this primitive man had no concept of testing another person to see what he could do. Nor was the idea of pure scientific curiosity one that he could accept easily. "But why do they want to know what colors we can see?" he asked over and over again. I think he finally accepted my explanation that they simply wanted to know for the sake of knowing as being another of the inexplicable things Mahars did. "They are Mahars, not men," he sighed, "and no one can understand them." I tried to explain that in my world men did similar studies for similar reasons, but he couldn't believe it.

In the lower corridors of the building I had to send Varna away, much to her disgust.

"Whatever they are plotting," she said, "you will have to let me in on it sooner or later."

"Of course," I replied, "but let me gain their confidence first. Besides," I added, "it's likely that this meeting will turn out to be dull and perfunctory, since it's my first contact with Elak's group."

At first, this prediction appeared to be all too true. Elak introduced me to three other men besides Tarmash. Two were pale "city people" and one was a thin man with dark hair and a copper colored skin. They regarded me with obvious suspicion, but Elak and Tarmash assured them that my behavior had been exemplary since I had been in the building. The others were all from other buildings, for all the parts of the city communicated with one another by numerous tunnels and passageways.

The business of the meeting was disappointing. The "red" man, whose name was Amrock, worked in the large central kitchens. His cohorts requested some lengths of glass tubing from those of us in the laboratory building. These were to be used in the distillation of some sort of alcoholic potion they were fermenting in vats in the back of the slave kitchens. A great deal of time was spent, it seemed to me, on the details of how much tubing was needed and exactly how it was to be bent and shaped. The only interesting thing that occurred was that one of the men produced, from a pouch at his hip, what appeared to be sheets of paper, and the specifications for the still were worked out on it with a charred bit of stick. I requested to examine the writing material. It did seem like thick paper—made from plant fiber of some sort, obviously, pressed into sheets and probably bleached white. I kept a sheet of it and returned the rest to its owner. No one questioned me, and shortly thereafter the meeting broke up.

Back in my own quarters I smoothed out my paper on the stone floor with Varna's help and set about composing a note to my Mahar captors. Varna made up an ink from bits of burnt sticks she obtained somewhere in her cleaning duties. I drew a diagram of the maze I had just been tested with and then a picture of a human figure looking at two globes, one of which we stained red with berry juice. I then labeled these drawings in English—"maze," "food," "man," "red light," etc. There is no written language in Varna's world, so I had to use English. I was sure the Mahars had some kind of written records—it was inconceivable to me that they could conduct experiments and keep records without it. And what about the problem of publishing results? A Mahar script was a certainty, but I had no experience with it. I could only leave the "note" in the test box and hope that English looked enough like Mahar that the reptilian scientists would see the resemblance and jump to the correct conclusion that I wanted to write to them.

It was with nervous anticipation that I returned to the test box on the next visit. When the door was opened and I stepped in I was at first bitterly disappointed. The sheet of paper lay where I had left it at the end of the last session! I picked it up. It was blank! In addition, there was a small hard stylus of graphite on the stone floor. The Mahars had not had the courtesy to answer my letter, but they had provided me with pencil and paper to write another!

How carefully I tried to compose that letter to the pterodactyl-like creatures who held me captive! Sitting in the small bare stone chamber in my ragged cut-off jeans, I laboriously set out to teach them English. I knew they must have a written language, but to convince them to teach it to me I needed to impress them with the fact that I already understood the concept of a written symbolic means of communication.

I drew a little sketch of a man and labeled it MAN. Then I illustrated ONE MAN and TWO MAN. (I decided not to go into the complication of spelling created by the plural form.) Reducing my "man" to a stick figure, I went on to illustrate numbers up to ten and then stopped. I learned later that this caused considerable interest in my audience, because they automatically work with a base of twelve. Then I wrote TWO PLUS TWO IS FOUR and illustrated with dots, and FOUR LESS TWO IS TWO. By that time I had pretty well filled the paper. I wrote large, having no idea how good Mahar eyesight might be. At the end of the trial I left the paper on the floor of the little chamber and was escorted back to the slave levels in the basement.

"Christopher!" cried Varna. "What happened?" I described my attempts to make contact with the Mahars.

"And if you do get them to write to you, what will come of it?" she questioned. "They are still Mahars—they have no interest in us except as slaves or food."

"Not so," I protested, "the very experiment Tarmash and I are engaged in—involuntary, I admit—shows that they are interested in knowing more about us, what we can do, how we think. If I can communicate with them I can set that research forward a hundred years!"

"Oh, Chris," she sounded exasperated, as she shook her head so that strands of her beautiful glossy black hair fell over her pretty face. "Oh, Chris, I think you are more interested in the Mahar's experiments than you are in getting us out of here and back to the tribe of Val-an!"

I rushed to seize her in my arms. I held her in a long embrace—she yielded, then I felt her little body stiffen against me. "Darling, what is it?" I whispered into the ebony cloud of her hair. She pulled away, her shoulders shaking. There were tears in her eyes, but she was shaking with laughter. "What is it?" I asked again.

"You slizak!" she said, trying hard to sound angry. A slizak is a small rock-crawling iguana sometimes kept by the cave children as a pet. They are not noted for their beauty or intelligence, and I'm sure the word is not used as a compliment. "You really are, aren't you?"

"What?" I asked stupidly. Of course, I was interested in the Mahar scientists and their experiments.

I was a scientist myself. Here was an opportunity to get into communication with another intelligent species. To date, in my own world, only some frustrating experiments with dolphins had even approximated such a thing!

"You only care about your stupid experiments, you care nothing about me!" my tearful lady exclaimed. "I can't stand this gloomy place! I spend all my time in tunnels and stone rooms. I never get to see the sun, I never feel the wind on my face. My skin is getting pale and ugly. And you—you enjoy it—you are having fun! You don't care if we ever get out!" She flung herself, now weeping openly, into my arms again. Well, I know only one way to calm a woman who feels she has been neglected or ignored. I lifted Varna in my arms and carried her into our rocky chamber.

Some time later, as I lay with my sleeping darling's head pillowed on my left shoulder, I considered the problem of escape. Making a rush for the exits from the underground city would probably get us to the surface, but how would we escape detection from the watch towers? Was there any other way out of the city? Well, there must be a drainage system, since the laboratories upstairs were said to have running water ("a spring in each cave"). And, of course, there was the way we had gotten in— fly on the back of a giant thipdar! That idea really intrigued me, I must ask Elak about the thipdar stables. I fell asleep and dreamed of sitting in a small Skinner box pounding the keys of a typewriter instrument which wrote on an endless belt of paper that rolled out of the box through a narrow slit where it was inspected by a committee of winged reptiles who were waiting for me to produce the works of Shakespeare.

VII

THE SCIENTISTS

The laboratory of the Mahar psychologists was huge. The roof arched overhead, supported by pillars of stone that rose from the smoothly polished floor. Along one side of the room were the training boxes, such as the one I had been in, eight to ten feet square, each "manned" by a winged reptile observer. Each was equipped with a bank of lights, a lensed periscope, and racks of colored filters in wooden frames as well as other apparatus I did not recognize.

I was led by my two giant pterodactyls to the other side of the chamber, past racks and cabinets of enigmatic boxes and instruments. On one wall was a chart which I realized with a start was a three color representation of the human brain. My escorts stopped at a desk-like apparatus with a set of translucent panels, probably bone, set into it, a pad of writing material and a now familiar stylus. There was no chair, since these creatures themselves could not sit but only perch.

One of the Mahars went around behind a paneled screen, the other motioned to me with its bizarre wing-fingers to step up to the desk. One of the panels lit up with a diffuse light and I saw upon it a well-drawn picture of a man. The other panel came alive. On it was a squiggly line and three dots and a dash. My heart leaped. They were going to teach me their written language! I had been right, they must have written records, although they could not speak, no matter how they communicated telepathically. Eagerly, I seized the stylus and made a notation on the pad. My lesson had begun. The reptile behind me flapped its huge wings and leaped to a perch atop a stone rail where it could look over my shoulder. Each time a set of pictures and "words" appeared, it pulled one of a series of knotted cords hanging from the ceiling. Somewhere a counter was keeping score.

Soon I began to get multiple choice questions: one picture and five possible words, or one word on the right-hand panel and four or five drawings on the left. I indicated my choice by pointing. When I was correct, the problem went off and a new one appeared. When I made an error, the lighted panels went off briefly and then came on again, and I got another guess. This process kept on for hours until I interrupted it by drawing the symbols for "food" and "water" on my note pad and showing them to the Mahar behind me.

The creature went off briefly and returned with fruit, nuts and water in an earthenware jar. While I ate, the other creature appeared and the two conferred. At least it seemed they did, standing on the polished stone floor, heads cocked toward each other, occasionally nodding or wiggling their winged fingers. Not a sound was made.

What were they doing? It did seem that they were all deaf. The room was quiet but there were noises as the other creatures working the observation boxes moved about, and on one occasion, a Mahar dropped a set of glass plates with a crash. None of the others turned to look at him, although my head turned almost automatically. Obviously the strange beings used some "sixth sense" to communicate with each other. I remembered that in the waters and skies of my own outer world there were animals that used ultrasound frequencies and electrical fields for communication and the location of their prey. I wished I had the instruments to explore the air between the two Mahars before me, because it seemed obvious that something was passing between them. Was it high frequency sound, X-rays, magnetic fields? The possibilities were endless. I determined that while they continued to study me, I would study them.

We returned to my language lesson and kept on until I had a hesitant vocabulary of nearly 300 words. I then had to ask to be allowed to sleep. Interestingly enough, I had no written Mahar word for this, perhaps the creatures did not sleep themselves. I had to resort to pictures and then pantomime and, finally making myself understood, I was led away by a Sagoth and returned to my quarters. There I told a fascinated Varna and Elak of my adventures. Elak, in particular, was interested.

"The Sagoths become more difficult, Red Axe," he said, "they demand more work of us and beatings have been frequent. Several of the laboratory workers and the garbage collectors have been chosen for the great games and for the secret rites of the Great Ones in the Temple. Previously, these jobs gave us protection from death in the arena, the temple, or the pits. Now several new Sagoths have been put in charge of the slave quarters. If you could complain directly to the Great Ones themselves by this new thing they are teaching you to do, it would perhaps save many of us."

I promised to learn the language as soon as possible and even to teach it to others. My friends were discouraging about that, however, for no tribe in all of Pellucidar has a written language. The idea was foreign to them both.

That was the beginning of what must have been

many weeks of time by outer world standards in the "class room." I am not a particularly good language student and progress was slow. One thing that puzzled me for quite a while was that the same symbols kept occurring in the words for entirely different concepts. I had assumed that a telepathic race would devise an ideograph for each thought or for each related thought. The squiggly line of the word for gilak or man, however, appeared as part of the word for "running water", "turn left" and "the color green." It finally dawned on me that the symbols represented syllables or "sounds" of some sort, and whatever form the Mahar telepathy took it involved the perception of sensations, not direct thoughts. It made me ever more curious about the so-called telepathic sense of the Mahars. It was also possible for me to assign sounds to the symbols to make them roughly correspond to the words of the Pellucidarian language. This was sometimes impossible, but I began to accumulate two "dictionaries" of notes—one Mahar-English and the other Mahar-Gilak. Varna was able to master some of the latter. As a matter of fact, it seemed easier for her to learn Mahar script than the English for her own spoken language.

I was the only one of us to achieve real communication with our captors, however. I did this mostly by doing "homework" of short essays which I wrote out and brought to the laboratory. These were usually in answer to questions put to me by the Mahars. For example, the first was an explanation of my ability to read and write when no gilak or Sagoth before me had been able to do so.

"In the place of my own tribe," I wrote, not having a Mahar word for "world" or "country", "almost every gilak can read. This art was developed many generations ago." Mahars did measure time, but, of necessity, they did so in biological terms. A long period of time was a Mahar life span, a gilak life span much shorter. A gilak sleep-period corresponded to a day, a meal-to-meal would be several hours, minutes were measured in breaths or heartbeats.

"In my place, gilaks live in cities like Mahars and have mastered the process of fast travel by machines, artificial light, communicating at great distances, and flying through the air."

The Mahars' response to this boastful report was predictable. "Why do the Mahars permit this to happen?" they asked.

"There are no Mahars at my place," I answered. "Creatures like the Mahars once existed, but they all died before the coming of the ancestors of the gilaks."

This brought a long, complicated reply from one of my interlocutors, whose designation was twelve twenty two mike, or something like that. All the Mahars had number-letter combinations for names. I was sure about the numbers, but, of course, "Mike" and "Zed", the two designations of my immediate Mahar companions, were merely my own words for the letter symbols of their names. All the reptiles who worked in the laboratory were twelve twenty two something, so that was probably a job designation. I referred to the two I worked with as "Mike" and "Zed." It was Mike who wrote the next, long communication. The gist of it was that, although the Mahars did not occupy the entire world ("space beneath the central sun"), they had never come in contact with city-building gilaks. Also, Mahars had never, in the many-generationed history of the race ("and a Mahar generation is many twelves of gilak births"), never died out in an area or withdrawn from one once settled there. Mike ignored my statement that where I lived there had never been any

Mahars. I think he assumed we must have learned to build cities from Mahars. Or, more likely, I had merely seen cities of the reptile people and was claiming my own folk could build them. He ended by asking me where I came from.

In reply, I brought to my next session in the laboratory a long dissertation on geography of the planet earth, the outer sun and the Solar System. They both read it carefully. These exchanges of information were always very time-consuming because we had to wait while they read what I had written and then wrote a reply, which I had to read, with frequent references to my dictionary, and then write a new reply. We sat at opposite ends of the work table. Or rather, I sat, having convinced my captors to make me a crude chair of stone. They both perched, like the great featherless birds they resembled, on rocks at the other side of the table. Each of us had a pad of paper and a stylus. When the "conversation" got hot, we would all three be scribbling furiously and passing notes back and forth like school boys in a study hall.

Zed commented that my view of the earth was very interesting but that it conflicted with that held by the Mahars. "You may not be aware," the creature wrote, "but there are ways of checking on beliefs such as this and ascertaining the true nature of things." Mike was more direct. "You have made all this up."

"I quite understand the scientific process of discovering the truth about natural phenomena," I wrote indignantly. "In my own place, I am a scientist myself, studying learning and perception in animals."

Zed looked at my paper and quickly penned me a note. "Perhaps you will tell me your ideas about color vision?" but Mike snatched it from me and

101

tore it up. Then I heard a Mahar make a sound for the first time, for Zed hissed at him and Mike hissed back! I doubt that they knew they were doing it. They confronted each other, their expressions unreadable, but obviously furious with each other, their heads weaving from side to side, hissing like a couple of boiling tea kettles. I watched, fascinated, for a while. I would greatly have liked to be able to listen in on their telepathic conversation, I figured Mike was bawling his companion out for revealing the nature of their study, or for trusting me at all.

I realized that here was a chance to make a friend, so I began writing furiously, beginning: "We believe that there are three units in the back of the eye that can see color. One for seeing red, one for blue, one for green (using the Mahar designations for the colors)." I passed this page across the table and began writing as fast as I could a description of the Young-Helmhotz theory of color vision. Zed picked up the first few pages, studied them a moment and then waved them in front of the still hissing Mike. After a while they quieted down and followed my dissertation with obvious interest, writing me a dozen questions, some of which I could not answer. Zed wanted to go on from there to discuss hearing, but Mike vetoed this, and I wrote that I was tired. Zed was a real enthusiast—he would have been willing to go on pumping me until I ran dry of information.

The next laboratory session began with my presenting my captors with a brief list of complaints made up by Elak—Sagoths were beating slaves without good reason, laboratory workers had been taken away to the arena and the pits and laboratory slaves were usually spared this fate, there had been no replacements for these workers so the slave force was shorthanded.

The two Mahars looked over my list. They perched side by side on the rocks at the end of the table and held the pages of stiff paper in their clawed feet, peering at it by turning their heads from side to side. Each of them bent over the table and wrote with their wing fingers on the pads of paper before them, ripped off the pages and handed them to me.

Zed had written, "This is very unfortunate. What can we do to help your fellow slaves?" Mike, on the other hand, had merely scrawled the Mahar equivalent of "So what?" on his page.

"Surely these things can be prevented by my powerful overlords," I replied. Bosses would have been a good word for them, but I did not have a Mahar equivalent except to invent a tiresome phrase like "one who supervises the work of a second person."

There ensued another silent conference between the two reptiles. I just knew that Zed wanted to promise to help me and Mike was against it. Finally, Zed wrote me a note which was obviously a compromise. Essentially, what it said was "we will look into it." Then he went on to ask for my dissertation on sound and hearing.

I produced the papers and handed them over. I had spent hours in my chamber below writing them out. It strained my knowledge of the Mahar language and my understanding of physics to explain sound waves to creatures who were deaf. I hastily wrote them another note and passed it over with the manuscript: "If any more slaves are taken away, I will stop writing what you ask."

Mike considered this a moment and wrote me a succinct reply, "Then you will be the first to go."

"The hell you say, buddy," I remarked aloud, knowing that they could not hear me. Indeed, they were already so deep into a perusal of my essay on speech and hearing that they did not notice me for the next hour or so.

Several interesting things came out of the interchange that followed. For one, the Mahars believed that the Sagoths who served them communicated entirely by sign language. They were shrewd enough to realize that movements of the face, especially the mouth, were important, but they had no idea of spoken speech. It was also apparent that they could not practice their telepathy, whatever it was, on Sagoths or humans—or any of the "lower species," they assured me. That was a relief, for I had sometimes wondered uneasily if they could detect my thoughts.

The theory of sound waves was entirely new to the two reptilian scientists. To prove the existence of sounds, I proposed that we build a microphone.

I was pretty sure they had electrical instruments of some sort because I had seen some in another lab. I had no word for electricity, however, and circuit diagrams are just that, diagrams. I didn't know the first things about the Mahar symbols for battery, coil, switch, resistance, voltage or what have you.

As a matter of fact, it took several sessions before we solved these problems. Mike and Zed got another Mahar to work with me. I never learned this creature's name. He always treated me with suspicion. I think he believed that I was a hoax, some kind of trick being perpetuated on him by his psychological colleagues. I suppose it seemed as incredible to him that I could read and write as it would have to me to be presented with a literate orangutan by a set of human scientists.

This new individual came to the lab equipped with a box of electrical parts and wires and a set of storage batteries in earthenware jars. With my help, he began to put together an experimental circuit. His wing fingers were amazingly dextrous, despite the clumsy crouch he had to get into to get them level with the table. The most surprising thing this creature did, however, was to reach into his tool kit and come out with a pair of huge, round glass lenses on a metal frame. These he carefully affixed to his long beak so that they were in front of his big reptilian eyes. I burst out laughing—fortunately, none of the Mahars noticed. Actually, I once had a high school physics teacher who wore a metal pince-nez that looked very much like the device the Mahar had on. This huge winged lizard, perched on his rock at the edge of the table, leaning over his experimental apparatus with his huge glasses positioned to his long-toothed snout, peering nearsightedly at my circuit diagrams, looked enough like old Mr. Ranligh to send me into uncontrollable giggles.

"Specs" was good at his trade, however bizarre his appearance. We built several carbon microphones and an apparatus for displaying the sounds picked up on a series of volt meters. I could easily design a microphone to pick up sound waves (a phenomena Mahar science was unaware of) and transduce them into electrical signals, but I was then hard put to know how to display the signal. In my own lab, I would have brought in an oscilloscope. Specs didn't have such a thing, however. He (or maybe I should refer to the Mahar individual as "it") was very interested in my description, and took it away to study. Subsequently, Specs may have startled the pterodactyl scientific world with his inventions—I never found out.

"Chris, are you sure it is a good idea to explain speech to the Mahars?" Varna questioned, "perhaps now that they know about it they can use the knowledge against us."

"Darling girl," I replied, "I've got to tell them something to convince them that I'm willing to co-operate with them. I don't see how it can hurt for them to know that their slaves are intelligent beings with a language."

"Perhaps," she said, "but from what I hear of the Mahars from the other slaves, I doubt it."

Whatever reservations Varna had, Elak was delighted. There had been a definite improvement in the treatment of the gilak slaves in our building. I asked Zed about it and he said, yes, the "animal psychology" laboratory had requested better treatment of all slaves, saying that the recent punishments and slayings had interfered with their research. "I had to maintain," he wrote to me, "that we were on the verge of some big discoveries, but I think your new science of acoustics, Red Axe, will convince the governing committee."

"Good," I wrote back, "when do you have to report?"

"Soon," was the reply, "in about twelve life times of a Ziggat." A Ziggat is a large dragon-fly insect who probably lives less than a day. Zed meant that a report of our research on sound was due in about a week. I went every "day"—that is, I spent much of my waking time between "sleeps" in the laboratory. It was before Mike and Zed presented their report, which was to be titled *Atmospheric Vibration Pattern, Used as Communication by Lower Species (Gilaks)*, that two events occurred that profoundly altered my relationship with the reptilian scientists.

The first was a sort of accident. Mike and Zed wanted to demonstrate sound to the review committee of scientists who would listen to their report of their work. Since no lower creatures would be permitted at such an important conference, they needed a noise maker. Specs and I had set up an electrical work bench at one side of the laboratory, and here I built a simple buzzer. When we first tried it, however, Specs leaped back from the bench as if he had received a shock.

I could not figure out what was the matter. The other winged reptiles in the room were agitated. They moved about the far side of the lab, looking in our direction. Several hurriedly left the room. Specs gestured to me wildly with his wing tip fingers and I disconnected the battery. The buzzer stopped and the Mahars visibly relaxed.

I was certain the Mahars had not heard the noise. Why had they reacted so violently? Specs proceeded to break down the buzzer and, with my help, build a speaker arrangement. He carefully took the interrupter out of the circuit and discarded it. That gave me my clue. It was the sparking of the contacts in the buzzer that had distressed the pterodactyl creatures—they were sensitive to radio static! Undoubtedly, this meant that their "telepathy" was some form of radio-sense!

This revelation struck me so forcibly that I sat staring at the apparatus and Specs had to shake me with his claws to get me back to work.

At the end of that "day" I shared my discovery and elation with Varna and Elak. "It means I may someday be able to speak to them directly and to listen in when they speak to each other," I said. I suddenly realized how difficult this was going to be; in all the electrical gear Specs and I had been working on, I had seen nothing like a vacuum tube. How was I going to build a receiver and a transmitter without tubes or transistor?

"We'll have to get back to the Had-bar caves for the supplies I need, though," I said.

Varna's pretty face broke into a smile. "At least, Christopher, my man, you see the importance of our escape."

"Elak," I said, "the water flows through this building must go into a main underground river somewhere in the city. Do you know where it is?" With the albino's help, I began drawing a map of the city of Phuma on the rock floor. There was a main drainage canal through which flowed all the sewage of the city, but it was several buildings away and Elak had never seen it. I suddenly realized how very restricted the lives of the slave people must be. Here was a man who had never been more than five hundred yards from the place where he was born.

"Those who collect the garbage from our building will know more, Red Axe," the pale man volunteered.

Of course, and I knew who that was!

Several "sleeps" later I accosted Gash as he left the common dining room.

"Come with you? Why should I do anything for you?" he challenged.

"Listen, short and ugly," I replied in English, "if I didn't need your help, I would be happy to take you apart limb by limb."

"What does that mean?"

"It means that my plans have become so complex and difficult that there is no one except Gash the Had-bar intelligent enough to understand or to help me," I replied, smiling.

"That's better," he grinned. "Let us go to your cave and talk. Your mate can wait on us."

My mate was more likely to kick him right in the rear, and me, too, for bringing him home, but I agreed. Fortunately, Varna was out. I showed Gash my plan of the city and the sewer. Gash saw the wisdom of my plan and promptly announced that he had thought of it himself.

"This river is open here, Red Axe," he said, pointing to my map, "where we dump the trash into it, but here," indicating with a dirty finger, "it flows under the rock into a cave. It is said that it comes out into a great swamp somewhere beyond, but none of the city people have seen that."

"Is there air above the water level in the tunnel? Could we swim through it?" I asked.

"There is a low roof but some breathing space at the opening," the cave man replied, "but it is dark, one can not see far in. The tunnel may be under water all the way. And we have no way of knowing how long it is." There was wisdom in that, I thought.

We were still considering ways to use the sewage tunnel when Varna burst into the room. "Christopher, come quick!" she cried, with barely a glance of disdain for my guest. "Tarmash is back from the laboratory. He has been gone for three sleeps. They have taken out his eyes! He is blind!"

VIII

ESCAPE

I pushed my way through the little crowd grouped around Tarmash. The pale man's lids were closed and sunken. A closer inspection showed the eyelids to be sewn shut. He sat dejectedly on the stone floor of the corridor, his mate beside him, weeping quietly. I talked to him—the group around us was very quiet, only a few whispers and the shuffling of bare feet on the rock as the man told his story. It was brief. They must have anesthetized him. He had no memory of anything beyond entering the laboratory maze as he did every "day". When he came to, he could not see. At first he thought he was in a dark room and he was very thirsty. He found his way around by feel. Then a Sagoth came for him and he realized that the ape-man could see and he could not. He had no pain but he seemed in a state of psychological shock.

And all the time the man was telling his story a voice in the back of my head was saying, "Of course, you might have expected it. This was an experiment on color vision, remember? They would need the eyes. They would want to examine the visual pigments, the histology, to correlate it with the behavioral data." I had a mental picture of the two Mahars, Zed and Mike, somewhere above us in the underground building, crouched over giant microscopes, looking at pieces of Tarmash's retina, talking to each other in reptilian pseudo-telepathy.

I patted the wounded man's shoulder and turned

away. My mind had gone cold and hard and frozen. "What is it, Christopher? What happened to him?" It was Varna. As I started to explain her pretty eyes widened with terror. "You," she cried, "they'll do it to you next!"

"Not yet," I replied, "they need me for the sound study for a while yet. Before that, my darling, we're going to get the hell out of here!"

I returned to our room with Varna and the Had-bar, Gash. Others in the crowd helped Tarmash's mate to lead him to their part of the corridors. Despite my quick reassurance of Varna, I felt a chill run up my spine. I was very probably scheduled for the same fate the poor slave had suffered! I resumed my discussion of escape with Gash.

The ugly Had-bar felt that he could possibly swim underwater far enough to escape. He doubted that we could keep up with him, but I suspected that he was bragging as usual. My own swimming ability I trusted, and I also knew that Varna could swim like a fish. She and I had spent many hours in the deep streams and pools of her native mountains. I tried to think of some way to construct scuba gear, explaining this to Varna and Gash. Gash was interested and at once saw the advantages of "carrying air in a bag." He knew of another building where pieces of metal were burned in bright flame and he described what might be welding. I told him to try to steal some of the tanks he had seen in that room. Varna and I would work on face masks. These we could construct from glass and rubber tubing which we knew to be available. Then I had to go off to the laboratory for the "day". Varna would try to get some glass jars which we might use as face plates.

I entered the laboratory with considerable trepidation, but only Zed and Specs were there at the time. Specs was anxious to start work on another microphone and electrical motor circuit, but I refused and made a hurried accusation to Zed, describing the events that had just taken place in the slave quarters, except, of course, that I left out any mention of our plans for escape. Looking about the laboratory, I had already spotted some rubber hose that looked useful, and I determined to steal some pieces of it soon as I could.

Zed answered me with a frank note, scribbling clumsily on the paper with his wing-fingers and then handing me the message with a taloned foot.

"Certainly, Red Axe," he wrote, "in your own world you sometimes sacrifice your experimental animals? We have done no more. As a matter of fact, we have spared the life of this particular subject, although I must admit we did so largely to use him in a subsequent experiment in which we plan to compare vision with the use of this new auditory sense you have taught us about."

That was no particular consolation to me! Or to Tarmash either, really. Nor was Zed's next note.

"Have no fear," he wrote, "you are far too valuable to our experiments for us to consider removing any of your organs at the present time."

That was all they would say about it! They had no intention of vivisecting me "at the present time!"

When Zed left, I found an opportunity to cut several sections of flexible tubing and slip them on my leg like bracelets. Specs seemed to take no notice. We continued our work on the microphones, and when I left I was still wearing the pieces of hose.

Varna had managed to get the bottoms cut out of several glass jars and we rubbed the cut glass smooth on the stone floor of our cell, and fitted the glass discs into the soft tubing. By trimming the opposite ends to fit our faces we produced three serviceable face masks which we could fasten on with leather straps. They would probably leak, but I hoped that we would need them for only a few minutes at most.

After the next day's meal Gash reported in. He said he had been able to steal two metal tanks from the welding shop and had hidden them near the underground river.

"Good," I said, "then we had better try our face masks during the next sleep period before we are all expected back to work. I only wish we had weapons of some sort. I hardly relish the idea of coming out of the river in the wilderness with no way to protect ourselves."

"I have weapons," said Gash. "I have hidden them in my cave because I knew some day I would try to escape."

"Good," I said, "go and get them."

He returned in a few minutes, furtively entering the room with a rolled furry hide in his arms. This he unrolled, revealing two stone knives and, to our surprise, my red fire axe!

"Gash, where did you get that?"

He grinned, his big ugly face almost splitting in half. "I stole it from a storeroom in this building," he said, "I could have taken spears and stone axes, but they would have been hard to hide. "Nah!" he cried as I picked up the axe and stuck it through my thong belt, "I get to keep that!"

"Now listen, Gash," I said, "you have been very helpful up to now, but you need me to show you the new way to swim underwater. Let's not fight until we have escaped from Phuma."

"And let's escape immediately and you men quit arguing," pleaded Varna. "Chris, take that axe out

113

of your belt and hide it in a bundle as Gash has done with the knives. We've got to walk out of here as if we had business to attend to."

The cave man and I glared at each other a moment and then we obeyed her. It is always difficult to argue with a beautiful woman, especially when she is right.

We started down the corridor, each carrying a bundle of hides, sticks and other trash, in which we concealed the knives, the axe and the face masks. We had no trouble inside our own building, we met only other slaves who either recognized us and gave a disinterested greeting, or ignored us altogether. At the doorway of the building, however, was an armed Sagoth who stopped Gash, who was in the lead, with a gesture.

"Hey, gilak, where you going?" he grumbled.

"I didn't get all this cleaning done," lied the Hadbar, grinning like an idiot. "I have to carry this stuff out."

"Go ahead," said the man-ape. "No, wait, what do you need them for?" he gestured at us with his club.

"They are helping me."

"There's not that much to do," said the Sagoth, looking at our puny bundles. "Here, you," to me, "you go help him, the she stays here with me." He picked the bundle from Varna's arms and added it to mine. For a moment I didn't know what to do. Gash continued on out of the building.

"Come ahead, Red Axe," he called. It seemed all our plans were dashed if I could not get Varna out of the building. The big Sagoth turned his back to me and leaned over her.

"You wait here with Ug-Lak, little one," he leered. I looked around quickly. There was no one else in the corridor or at the door. I put my bundle

114

quietly on the ground and drew out the axe. For a moment I considered trying to stun the brute with the blunt end, but then decided against it. If I was going to hit him at all I must disable him on the first blow. I struck with all my might at the base of his skull. With a groan he crashed to the floor. I wiped the axe on his shaggy coat and Varna caught up the bundles.

"Quick, Christopher," she whispered. We spotted Gash ambling on some distance away and hastened to catch up. Slaves and Mahars and a few armed Sagoths passed us. I wanted to run—it might be only minutes before the body of the dead Sagoth was discovered—but to maintain our disguise we had to stroll slowly, as if we had all the time in the world.

"You shouldn't have done that, Red Axe," commented Gash, "better to have left the she behind."

"Gash," I replied in the same conversational tone he had used, "the ladies of my world would consider you the worst kind of male chauvinist."

"I don't know what that means," the ugly fellow grunted.

"I'll tell you what it means," said Varna. "It means you better not turn your back on me the next time I have a spear in my hand."

"However," I reconsidered, "if anyone has a right to be a male chauvinist, it's a real red-blooded Neanderthal cave man."

"You both talk too much." observed Gash. We proceeded on for another ten city blocks, passing several of the hideous Mahars, none of whom paid us the slightest attention. I could hear the rushing of the river.

The garbage dump was deserted, at least temporarily. The river was wide and the current did not look too fast. A series of broad steps cut out in the rock led down to the water. It looked deep. The water came out from under a large, windowless building that rose to the roof of the cavern. Some ten yards farther on the stream passed into a rough, rounded tunnel in the rock wall.

"Gash," I requested, "go get the gas tanks, the heavy things from the fire room. We will wait here."

"I go," he agreed, "and if any Sagoths come along, pretend to be resting."

Fortunately, no one chanced near, and Varna and I slipped into the water and tried the facemasks. We had brought a length of rawhide strap and we cut pieces of this to tie the rubber masks to our faces. The glass was irregular and pitted, the images were distorted, but the mask permitted some vision in the dark water. We dove repeatedly beneath the surface. The river was only five or six feet deep, the bottom covered with broken pottery, glass and stone rubble thrown into it by the garbage detail.

I investigated the outlet of the river and found a narrow ledge just within the mouth of the cavern. It was not a safe hiding place but it sheltered us partially from the eyes of any passerby. Varna and I transferred all our paraphernalia there before Gash returned.

I waited for him at the edge of the garbage dump, hidden in the dark flowing waters, with just my head exposed. When a pair of armed Sagoths strolled by, I held my breath and submerged. I can stay under water more than a minute, and I kept myself down until my lungs cried out for air, then cautiously raised my masked face 'til it was level with the water's edge and peered about. The coast was clear and soon Gash came ambling down the stone steps carrying two cylindrical metal containers about two feet long and eight or ten inches in diameter, one painted green, the other red. After a few hurried words of instruction, we swam with his prizes under the cave overhang and deposited them on the ledge.

At first I thought Gash's theft might turn out to have been all in vain, for I could not discover how to open the tanks and let the gas out. If it took some special wrench or other tool, we were out of luck. I did not dare risk another expedition into the city—by now the body of the Sagoth guard I had murdered must surely have been discovered.

At last, however, I found that twisting the top of the cannister released a stream of gas under pressure. At the same time, we also found that one of our cylinders was useless, for the gas rushing from it stunk like rotten eggs—it was obviously not oxygen, or air, nor was it breathable in any concentration. I quickly turned it off and tried the other— the gas was odorless and a lung full of it did me no harm. Probably oxygen, I decided.

I had no tubing or proper scuba gear. The best I could improvise was to carry the gas cannister with me in my arms underwater and inhale from it by pressing my mouth to the funnel-shaped escape jet. This was a technique I doubted my companions could easily master.

"I will go ahead downstream with the gas can," I said to Varna and Gash, "and see how far we must swim to get out of the tunnel. Then I will swim back to you."

"Oh, Christopher, do not leave me," cried my dark-haired maiden. "I fear if you disappear down that dark river I will never see you again."

"Darling," I said, holding her slim little hand in mine, "I will go only a short way, test the gas and return. If I can find no exit, I will come back to you, rest and try again." So I persuaded her. Gash was perfectly content to let me take the initial risks while he sat on the ledge under the dark overhang.

I took a deep breath and dove. The weight of the gas cannister helped drag me down toward the bottom and I paddled downstream into the darkness. Rapidly the tunnel became pitch dark. I raised a hand above my head, but quickly met rock. Breathing from the cannister was difficult and it was hard not to panic alone there in the dark, completely underwater. My second try, however, revealed an air pocket above me and I surfaced and could breathe. The echos of my splashing suggested that I was in a fairly large cave and I let the current of the river carry me along, for, best of all, there was a glimmer of light ahead.

This proved only to be a beam of light from a shaft high in the roof. Treading water, I slipped off the face mask. My eyes adjusted to the gloom, and I could see that the stream I rode disappeared again under the far wall of the cave. However, it was a hiding place with air, and not far from the entrance. I was reasonably sure my companions could swim it underwater without the oxygen tank, for I had proceeded cautiously and slowly on my way in, not knowing there was light and air ahead. As soon as I had rested, I returned to them, making the return swim upstream without using my reserve air supply.

Varna and Gash were delighted to see me, especially the former, and glad to hear my news. We lost no time in evacuating the partially exposed ledge with all our weapons and paraphernalia and making the quick underwater swim to the hidden cavern. Here we again found a semi-dry space to cache our goods while I took the oxygen cylinder and made yet another exploratory dive.

This was a longer swim in the cold and the dark,

and its results were bitterly disappointing. I came to a grating of timbers lashed together with rope or hide thongs. Exploring clumsily with my free hand, it seemed that the obstruction completely blocked the passage. Cold and exhausted, I took a breath from my auxiliary tank and began the long swim back in the dark. As I did so, I felt something that made my blood freeze with apprehension. Across my bare thighs I felt, a slow, slimy sinuous touch. Some serpentine denizen of the dark, fully as round as my leg, by the feel of it, brushed against me for a moment, then was gone.

Back in the cavern with Varna, I explained to her, and to Gash, the nature of our predicament. "We should have anticipated there would be some sort of protection device at the end of the sewer system, if only to keep enemies from entering the city." I thought of the thing that had touched me in the water and shuddered.

"What can we do now?" asked Varna. We were clinging to the rocky side of the cave close to where the lone light shaft entered from the eternal noonday sun without. The sun beam penetrated the murky water only a few feet, but by its reflected illumination we could see around us. We had piled our belongings among the rugged rocks, and Varna had perched herself among them, her bare feet trailing in the water. Gash and I clung to the side of the cavern, resisting the current with occasional strokes of the arms or legs.

"I may be able to cut some of the timbers loose with my axe," I replied. "It would help if I could see. Perhaps I can ignite the other gas can Gash brought." The green cannister had been conveyed into the cavern with the other supplies. "Is there any way to strike a light?"

"I can get a few sparks from striking two of the

stone knives together," Varna replied, "but how are you going to get anything to burn in a water-filled tunnel?"

"I may be able to bend the gas jets of the two tanks together and make an oxy-acetylene torch out of them," I said. "Anyway, it's worth a try." I began working with the tanks while my companions rested in turn upon the rocks.

I was able to ignite the gas from the green cylinder with a spark. It burned with a yellow, smoky flame. Binding the two cylinders together, I tried to get the nozzles close enough to mingle the gas streams. I had no idea how much gas was left in each container, and I dared not use too much in experimenting.

As I was struggling with the metal nozzles, my blood was chilled by a gasping cry behind me. "Christopher, help!"

I turned quickly, seizing my axe from the rocks. Varna was some ten feet from me in the gloom and as I turned she seemed to draw away still further from the ledge. Her eyes were wide with terror, but for the moment I could not see why. Then she rose up out of the water slightly and I could see two coils of grey flesh, each a foot thick, encircling her below the waist!

With a shout I threw myself towards her in the water, grasped her with my left arm. My darling never said a word after her first cry to me. She struggled with her little hands against the hideous tentacle that held her.

Seizing a loop of the creature, I struck downward into it with the axe. The water impeded the force of my blow, but the flesh was soft. Again and again I struck, and then the beast reacted. The coils loosened and pulled away and I dragged Varna free. At the same moment something surged to the surface yards away and loomed up in the darkness, the water rushing off of it in rivulets. It had a huge head, at least eight feet high, with gigantic eyes that reflected the light of the single illuminating sun beam so that they seemed to glow in the murk.

The water between us and the monster boiled with flailing tentacles. In the center of the huge head a beak-like mouth opened and emitted a piercing whistle. The gigantic thing began to move towards us in the water. A tentacle grasped the rocks near us as Varna and I scrambled up on the side of the cavern. I swung the axe again, severed the tip of the grasping thing as two more coils came up out of the water onto the rock. Chop! and again chop! went my blood smeared axe. Once more the thing was slow to react, but when it did it hooted in pain or anger and withdrew from the ledge. It sank so that the great glowing eyes were half submerged, but it did not flee. It seemed to float there as if contemplating the best way to accomplish our capture. I looked around for Gash. The poor fellow had climbed half way up the rock wall, clinging by the barest finger and toe holds, but he had reached an impasse and there he hung, almost gibbering with fright.

Varna seized her flint knife and crouched ready at my side. Together we watched the silent kraken-like creature, wondering if it would retreat having found that we were no easy prey. Maybe, I thought, it was afraid of fire. I pulled the gas tanks over to me, and with fumbling wet hands, struck sparks from our flint knives until I had ignited the gas jet from the green cannister. The orange flame did little to light the cave, and it made a plume of thick choking smoke. The pressure seemed to be lower than it had been a few moments before.

"Christopher!" hissed Varna's voice beside me, "it comes!"

I twisted the top of the oxygen tank, the two gases mingled, the flame grew brighter. I lifted the ignited torch above my head and stood up. The creature kept right on coming for me. A tentacle like a tree trunk flashed out of the water and encircled me at the hips, raised me into the air. In front of me I saw that beaked maw opening between hideous glowing eyes. The touch of the thing was cold and slimy. In desperation I drew back the gas cylinders and hurled them, still flaming, into that gaping orifice. The hard beak closed on them with a crash of rendering metal, the face of the monstrosity was briefly enveloped in a puff of flame.

With an anguished screech the beast let me slip from its tentacles into the water, thrashing the surface with its many limbs. The flames had been instantly extinguished, but as my eyes readjusted to the dim light, I saw the bulk of that huge ungainly head sink below the surface. Quickly I struck out for the rocky ledge.

"Christopher, do you think you have slain it?"

"No, I doubt it very much. It may stay down for a while—at least, I hope so. Come on, let's not sit here in the dark waiting for it to come back and pick us off. Back upstream!"

We started for the overhead that marked the underwater passage back to the city of the Mahars.

"Gash, are you coming with us?" I called.

"I do not intend to let you leave me behind to be eaten by the underwater creature," he replied.

"Very well," I said, steadying myself on the edge of the cavern with a hand. "You go under first, then Varna. I will guard our rear in case the monster pursues us."

The river swept under the rock with a firm pressure, but the distance was not great to the garbage dump on the other side, and I was sure we could all make it with little trouble. I pushed Gash under, waited a minute, and motioned Varna to follow. With a brave smile she pulled her face mask over her eyes and nose, took a breath and dove.

I looked back down the gloomy, watery cave. Our only hope of escape—blocked. Was there a serpentine thrashing at the far end of the cavern? I pulled my own mask into place and dove, holding my axe ready in one hand, although it impeded my swimming.

Almost immediately I could see light ahead. As I broke into the opening, however, I saw Varna's body directly ahead of me, treading water. I wondered why she had not landed. Then my head broke the surface and I saw seven big Sagoths standing on the landing. One of them held Gash none too gently by both arms. They pointed to me and to Varna and motioned us to swim to the shore.

IX

TEMPLE OF THE MAHARS

There was only one satisfaction about our recapture. The water behind us was suddenly disturbed by the thrashing of the huge tentacles of the dweller in the tunnel. In the ensuing confusion, you may assume that Varna and I got out of the water with alacrity. The cave girl managed to slip my steel-bladed axe under her brief hide garment. Varna was wearing a single animal skin, fur side out, which hung from one shoulder and encircled her hips. It was held together by rawhide thongs and a bead and shell decorated belt and inadequately covered her firm young breasts, but it was high fashion in the tribe of Val-an. Under this, she concealed my axe, and we scrambled out of the water amid the shouts of the surprised Sagoths and the monster in our wake.

So incredible was the vitality of our pursuer, that I almost expected it to come right up out of the river tunnel after us. The Sagoths seemed of a similar mind, for they gave back from the river bank with cries of alarm. A number of spears and stone axes were launched at the flailing tentacles, with no result. The monster, however, seemed to pause at the water's edge, the groping tentacles exploring the steps leading down to the river. There was no definite sign of the gigantic head and huge eyes. Perhaps the water was too shallow for it, for the creature then withdrew.

After making sure it was gone, the Sagoths hustled us off to a building I had never seen before. Up a long corridor and through an iron-barred gate into a large room where some twenty other humans sat or lay about the floor, dejected. The gate slammed behind us, and with a few gutteral words among themselves, the Sagoths left one of their number on guard and the rest departed.

I looked about our prison, for there was no need to pretend it was anything else. The chamber was high and about forty feet wide. The ceiling must have been at least another forty feet high, but the walls were irregular and about half way up one wall were two large slits in the stone, and through these came a diffuse light from the noon day sun of Pellucidar. The iron bars of the gate we had entered closed the only other exit from the chamber.

The men observed us listlessly. We noticed now that there were several women among them. All of them seemed sunk in deepest gloom. One man rose from the ground and approached. He was one of the pale city people. "Welcome, stranger," he said slowly. "Welcome to the chamber of sacrifice."

"What do you mean by that?" asked Gash. "I'm here by mistake. Actually, I was trying to prevent the escape of these two—as soon as the great Mahars realize that, I will be released."

"Oh, for God's sake, Gash," I said, helping Varna to a seat near the door and lowering myself down beside her. "Stop all that. Nobody here is interested in your stories."

Gash was offended. "Pay no attention to them," he assured the man who had spoken to us. "They do not know whereof they speak. I am Gash, the Mighty Had-bar, servant of the Mighty Mahars."

The pale man smiled slightly. "You must indeed be a loyal servant of the Mahars to be condemned to death in the temple," he said.

"What do you mean by that?" Varna asked quickly.

The man turned and looked over his shoulder. Several of the others had climbed up the wall on the far side of the chamber and were peering out of the illuminated slits in the stone.

"Akar," he called, "have they started yet?"

One of the bearded, fur-clad men at the window turned his head, "It begins," he replied.

"Come, strangers," said our interlocutor. "Come watch the Mahars at play. "You," he said to Gash, "may see something you did not know about the Great Ones."

We climbed with bare feet up the wall and found places where we could peer out. The slit-like windows were only about six inches high, too narrow to crawl through. The wall was another six inches thick; beyond this, we gazed into a huge domed chamber, illuminated by many shafts of sunlight falling through openings in the roof. Most of the floor of the chamber was covered with a lake of water which reflected the sunlight in brilliant patches on the walls. Scattered on the surface of the lake were four or five barren islands, really only bare rocks protruding from the water. Crowded on each of these were small groups of human beings.

They must have been able to see our window slits, perhaps even our faces, but their attention was directed elsewhere. They were gazing fixedly at a point below us where, because of the depth of the stone slits, we could not see. The people below were almost motionless, watching whatever lay below our wall with a fixity that bespoke only terror.

"Chris, what is happening to them?" asked Varna, taking my hand.

"Below us are the Mahars," said the man who had accompanied us to the windows. "You will see them in a moment." His voice was hushed, as if the terror of the people below us had infected him also. There was a gasp from the other watchers at the windows and we turned back. Below us, I could see the heads of four of the reptilian Mahars. To my amazement, they were swimming in the water. The great bat-like wings were only partially spread, the long pointed heads were held erect above the surface and they were paddling with their feet. Slowly, silently, they advanced on the rocky islands and their hapless, human inhabitants.

One of the weird creatures drew up opposite each of the islands and seemed to fix its gaze on one of the men and women clustered there. The bird-like heads protruded from the water a few yards from the shore, and the huge eyes entrapped a victim.

For a while nothing happened, but then I noticed that the Mahars were swaying their heads slowly from side to side. Horribly, one of the humans in each group also began to sway from side to side, keeping time with the reptilian creature before him. The other humans drew back from the entranced ones as they continued their swaying and began to walk toward their tormentors. There were two men and two women. They entered the water, walking slowly, their eyes fixed on those of the Mahars before them.

To my horror, I saw the reptiles withdraw farther into the water, drawing their victims hypnotically after them until they disappeared beneath the surface!

I turned to our informant. "Have they drowned them?"

He shook his head. "Watch," he said, and pointed across the indoor lake at a narrow sandy beach on the opposite side of the chamber. I watched, and sure enough, I soon saw the serrated back and beaked head of a Mahar appear dripping from the depths. The creature was walking backward and in a moment it had moved up onto the narrow shore. After it rose the head of one unfortunate cave man! Slowly he walked up onto the sand, his eyes fixed on his tormentor. The reptile led him up onto the sand and then, as another Mahar rose from the lake, the first turned, still walking backward, and again drew his victim into the depths. The second victim was a woman, and even at that distance, I could see the marks of the Mahar's toothed beak on her shoulders and breast!

I watched in utter disbelief as each of the four creatures repeated this performance and the first one reappeared. The man following his slow progress backward across the sand was now, however, missing an arm at the elbow! The wound did not even seem to be bleeding. He paid no heed to his mutilation but followed the pterodactyl again into the waters, to reappear minutes later with his other arm missing!

"My God," I gasped, "they're being eaten alive!"

All of the helpless humans now showed evidence of attack by the reptilian monsters. For the first victim, the end came soon. He was drawn hypnotically across the sandy beach once more, both his arms chewed off at the shoulder and part of his face and scalp missing. The waters closed over his mutilated head again and he never resurfaced. After a while, a Mahar rose in the waters and swam slowly away, and I assumed the poor wretch had been completely devoured in the depths.

More and more of the winged reptiles entered the waters of the underground lake and drew the unresisting humans from their pitiful rock perches to their grisly doom. I turned away, sick and weak with anger and horror. The man who had spoken to us earlier watched me, his face impassive.

"Does this . . . does this thing happen often?"

"About every three sleeps," he replied. "Sometimes they wait until there is a large number of us so that many of them may feed together. Those you saw killed just now were taken from this very chamber not long ago."

Varna clung to my arm, her head buried on my shoulder, too shocked to speak.

"Do they feed *us*, at least?" I asked.

"Yes," said my informant. "Who are you, that you do not know the Mahars eat gilaks?"

"I am Red Axe, of the tribe of Val-an. And this is my mate, Varna."

"I am Elkar, of the City of Phuma. I am sorry

128

to see you here in the death chambers of the Great Ones."

That was our welcome to the Mahar prison!

For a while, we just ate and slept like the rest of the prisoners. The apathy they displayed amazed me. None of them, with the exception of Gash, railed at his fate. Gash, of course, complained constantly and devised numerous schemes of escape—all of them ridiculous.

I talked to each of the men in the cell, Varna talked to each of the women. There were twenty-four of them, the three of us made twenty-seven. Many of the men were from outside tribes, proud, independent, barbarian peoples. They were all filled with anger and despair, but the idea of concerted group action had not occurred to them. If there were other members of their own tribe here, they assured me, they would all fight together like demons, but they could hardly be expected to trust men or women from other tribes!

The women, I must say, were well-treated by the men. Only one, other than Varna, had her mate with her. The men were a fierce-looking lot, hairy and bearded, clad only in loincloths, mostly bare-footed. Several of them were distinctly ape-like in appearance, hulking brutes, beetle-browed with stooping posture and long arms that reached almost to the ground. One tall, slender and graceful man, who said his name was Mooh-lah, had a long, pre-hensile tail!

Perhaps the possession of the axe, the only weapon in the cell, made me more aggressive than the others. Varna and I had hidden the axe under some rubbish in one corner of the room. I really think, though, that the rest of the poor cave men were so in awe of the monstrous Mahars that the thought of resistance had never entered their heads. I had the advantage of close association with the creatures, and I knew that no matter what strange things went on in the watery temple of horrors, the winged masters of Pellucidar were as fallible and as mortal as men. I had no intention of letting them eat me alive without putting up a fight. So I circulated among the cave men, talking and talking, trying to convince them that they should not submit to the terrors of the lake.

Elkar agreed with me, he was a born leader, and he undertook to convince some of the stupider Neanderthal types to give us their support. The tailed half-man, Mooh-lah, and two brawny cave men who reminded me of Varna's tribe, committed themselves to our cause. Before the next selection of sacrifices for the feed was made, we agreed that I should address the entire group, for our slim chance of success rested on the cooperation of all the humans. Elkar said usually a dozen Sagoths came for the victims, entering the prison and sorting out those who were to go. He had survived two such selections, now had no hope of being overlooked a third time.

"My mate and child were lost to me in the first group, before I knew what they were doing," he said. "I do not want to avoid the next selection, I wish only to avenge their deaths."

"Good," I told him. "Before the Sagoths come again we must have some semblance of a plan. If we get out of this building, where is the nearest entrance to the city?"

"Not far," he replied. "From this building is a major thoroughfare (he said 'much traveled path') and the cave entrance can be seen to the left. There is a long ramp going up, but it is usually guarded by many Sagoths and Mahars."

"Nevertheless," I assured him, "we must have something to offer the group."

"There are more gilaks imprisoned somewhere in this building or the one next to it," mused Elkar. "If we could locate them and turn them loose——"

"Good, we'll try it. I think the time has come to persuade the group."

I walked into the center of the room. The Sagoth guard at the cell door was asleep, sitting across the corridor from us. I motioned Mooh-lah to the door, where he kept watch.

"Fellow gilaks," I called, in a quiet voice. The men gathered around me. "It will not be more than a few sleeps before the Sagoths come to take some or all of us to a dreadful death in the lake below."

They looked at me dumbly. This was something they all knew. Surely, every waking moment, their minds were preoccupied with little else.

"Outside this prison cell, outside this building, outside this hideous underground city," I continued, "lies sunlight, open country and freedom! I know that no one has ever escaped from Phuma. I have tried, some of you here have tried. We got caught." Some of the men grunted assent. I had their interest now.

"We got caught because we were one or two men alone," I continued. "Never have a group of determined gilaks tried to fight their way to freedom. We are twenty-seven strong. When that gate opens, there will be a mere dozen Sagoths between us and the first step to escape. We will attack them and beat them to the ground——"

"We will be killed," grunted a big Neanderthal in the front row.

"*Some* of us will be killed," I agreed. "Some of us will be killed getting out of here, but some of us will get out. More of us will be killed getting out of the city, but Elkar says the entrance to the city is close."

"Very close, but guarded," said that worthy, cautiously.

"We will be killed," repeated my first heckler. His slow mind could deal with only one thing at a time. What he said was self-evident, but he could not get past it.

"You are right," I admitted, "but whether we fight or do not fight, we shall all be killed." This was really the big point of my speech, but some of my audience were not too bright, so I thought I'd better drive it home. "If we let the Sagoths take us, we shall all die a terrible, frightful death. If we fight, some of us shall die, but some Sagoths will also die, and there is even a chance that a few of us will win freedom. I will lead the attack on the Sagoths if you will all swear to follow me. We must all attack together; no man or woman can hold back. One way we die a terrible, helpless death under the cold waters of the lake. The other way we die a clean, fighting death, one we need not be afraid of. Nay, a few of us may not die but live to escape this terrible city!" Waxing overly eloquent, I shouted, "I know not what course others may take, but as for me, give me liberty, or give me death!"

A modest, and somewhat hushed, burst of applause greeted my assay into oratory. No one wanted to awaken the guard.

The guard was rudely awakened shortly thereafter, however, for the Sagoths arrived to conduct the sacrifices to the pool. The leader, a tall, heavy ape man, even among these brutes, kicked him sharply in the ribs. "Up, lazy! Open the cage! Time has come for the fattened gilaks," he cried.

The humans and half-humans in the prison cell

drew together and a murmur of fear swept them. "Courage," I whispered. "Varna, bring me the axe. The rest of you, pick up stones or bones and hold them behind you."

There was a rustle and a rattle as they obeyed. The iron gate clanged open and the big, leather-clad apes ambled into the chamber. My allies huddled together at the far wall, under the little window slits.

"Spread out! Each of you pick a man and strike when you hear me yell," I hissed. "Elkar, you and I will rush the leader and get through to the gate to be sure they don't shut it again. Ready!"

The Sagoths were armed with stone axes and knives, but these were stuck in their belts or hung loosely in their hands. They were not expecting trouble, but the entire group of ten of them entered the room. My hand tightened on my axe, my palms were wet with sweat. I wished for a moment to bend down and rub them in the dust on the floor. There was no time. The big leader stepped forward and gestured toward us with his fist. "You, and you," he said, his voice low and slow. He's probably just a big dumb lout, I thought, he's probably just doing his job. Then I didn't dare wait any longer.

"Now, gilaks! Strike!" I yelled. I leaped at the leader, producing my steel-bladed axe, its edge honed to razor sharpness with stones. A quick side-stroke half decapitated the brute and he fell, gushing bright red blood.

I reversed my stroke and my axe circled my head as I leaped over the body of my first victim. I saw Elkar stoop to seize his stone headed cudgel as my axe crashed into the head of the Sagoth behind him. Now, the underground chamber was filled with cries and shouts of alarm. The ape-men in front of me gave back a moment and then surged forward with a snarl of rage, drawing their weapons. Rocks flew past my head and another Sagoth went down. With Elkar on my left, wielding the stone axe, and Varna close behind on my right, I led my little, desperate band in a rush toward the door.

The Sagoths stood their ground. Cudgels rose and fell. I sidestepped a blow and chopped down on the arm that aimed it. The ape-man dropped his weapon with a howl, but seized me with his other hand. His huge fingers closed around my throat and I was lifted up from the ground, kicking and struggling. If the creature could have used his other arm, I would have been finished in a moment, but I had shattered the bone with my first stroke. Now, as the world began to go black before my eyes, I aimed a downward chop at his muscular shoulder. Luckily, I connected and the Sagoth had to drop me. I lay prone for a moment, dragging air back into my starved lungs, and then struggled to my knees. My opponent was down and three of the cave men were on him with rocks and captured stone knives. With both his arms crippled he gnashed at his attackers with his great white fangs.

Varna pulled me to my feet and I staggered erect, still clutching my blood-stained axe. Before us stood the open door of the cell, beyond the single guard, still groggy with sleep, stared at us unbelievingly.

"Come on," I cried, and rushed at him. Elkar, Varna and two others followed me into the corridor. The Sagoth guard turned and ran! In a moment, the slap of his bare feet faded down the dim passage. We were free! Free, at least for the moment, I looked back into the prison cell. Two Sagoths were still on their feet and, even as I watched, one was pulled down by his attackers. The last ape-man, however, had backed himself against the wall. His heavy stone-shod hammer whistled in a deadly arc before him, the efficiency of which was attested by the pile of bodies before him. His ugly face was contorted into a hideous grin, but he was, as yet, untouched.

"Red Axe, Red Axe," cried several of the crowd around the big Sagoth. Well, I thought, this is the price I pay for leadership. I shifted my grip on my axe and waded back through the press. The ape-man saw me coming and grinned more ferociously than before, were that possible. I paused, just out of his reach. He stopped swinging his huge club and held it ready. Around me the cave men pulled back as if to give me room.

I shifted the handle of my weapon in my fist. The big ape-man had the reach on me; the only way I could hit him was to get inside his guard. Getting in close to these fellows carried its own risks. My neck still throbbed from the last time I had closed with a Sagoth. The safest thing to do was get in, hit him a hopefully crippling blow, and get back out. The monster shifted easily on his feet, his little eyes fixed on my face.

"Elkar, Varna, Mooh-lah, anybody," I said under my breath. "Clubs, knives, whatever you've got, ready to throw at my command."

"Come on, little man," called the Sagoth, "come and get me!"

"Ready, Red Axe," said a voice to my rear. I dared not turn to look at my followers. The Sagoth and I were close, barely out of range. If I glanced aside, he would rush me and splatter my brains across the prison floor with that stone-headed club.

I drew a deep breath and picked my target—the shoulder and neck muscles of the arm that wielded the weapon.

135

"Now!" I cried. A barrage of captured Sagoth weapons flew through the air at my antagonist. Surprised, he let out a howl and raised both arms to protect his face. In a flash, I was in at him. The steel blade of the fire axe whistled in a short arc and chunked into the creature's neck and collar bone. He let out one quick grunt of pain. I was back out of range in a single bound, but a glance showed me that my opponent was disabled. The arm holding his stone axe, still clutched in his massive fist, hung at his side, his other hand clutched his wounded shoulder. I felt a stab of sympathy for the poor brute, but I didn't waste time on the finer emotions. I stepped back in and slammed the axe into his skull. Behind me, my fellow humans raised a little cry of triumph. The last of our immediate captors bit the dust.

"Grab the weapons," I directed. "Elkar, where are you?"

"Here, Red Axe," the pale cave man was close behind me with Varna. They were both unhurt. Close behind them was Gash, the Had-bar, and he also, I noted without much surprise, was unscathed.

"Red Axe, that was magnificent," Elkar's eyes glowed. "You slew four Sagoths all by yourself!"

"I had help," I grinned, giving Varna a quick hug, "and I sure needed it." My darling cave girl clung to me for only a moment. Her thick black hair had come unknotted from the thongs she bound it with in back, and stood out around her face in wild disarray. Her face shone with excitement and, like Elkar, she grasped a long sharp stone knife in her right hand. I pressed her body close to me and then released her.

"Which way to the street outside the buildings?" I asked Elkar, "we must move fast before the Sagoths realize what's happening."

He gestured and we started down a long dim tunnel. My little band made no noise, their naked feet and hide sandals quiet on the rock floor. Halfway down the corridor, we were halted by a cry from a side passage. Elkar turned to me, questioning. "It is another cell of gilaks," he said. "They must have heard the fighting and guessed that we are escaping."

I hesitated a moment. If we had any hope of escaping, it probably lay in reaching the surface before the Sagoths and their reptilian overlords could gather a force large enough to destroy or recapture us. On the other hand, I could not bear to leave human beings behind us, doomed to the unspeakable fate of the temple pool.

"Take three or four men and run and release them, if you can get the door open," I said. "We will remain here and hold the main corridor. Tell them to join us and fight or flee for their lives."

Elkar hurried to do my bidding. I was amazed at the ease with which I had assumed command of the jail break. The others—men and women— gathered around me. We rested, waiting.

It was not long. Our four were back, with them half a dozen men and women. "The others refused to come," Elkar reported, "they say it is against nature to dispute the will of the Great Ones."

"Let them stay down here and die, then," I spat. "We have no time for philosophical arguments." I glanced around at my pack. We were a sorry looking crew. Even with the new arrivals, we numbered less than twenty. We shared our weapons with the newcomers and hastened down the passage.

In a moment, we could see light ahead and we burst into the street, illuminated by shafts of sunlight from openings high above us in the roof of the cavern. There were only a few human slaves about and they promptly ran when they saw us. A big Sagoth guard came running out of a building but thought better of it and turned to flee. Before he could get away, though, he was tripped up by a thrown cudgel and a gang of my men fell on him with knives and dispatched him. His weapons were seized with cries of glee, and several of the rebels danced atop his corpse.

"Which way?" I demanded of Elkar, and he pointed up and towards the left. "Come on!" I cried. "To the city entrance and freedom!"

"Freedom!" cried some of my followers, and "Kill the Sagoths!" cried others.

"You'll probably get more of the latter than the former," I muttered to myself as we trotted up the street in the direction indicated by Elkar.

"What say you, Christopher?" Varna called at my side.

"I say that I would give a great deal for a couple of M-2 service rifles right now," I replied.

"Yes, and so would I," she said, catching the gist of my meaning. "Look, they advance against us!"

And, indeed, ahead of us was a party of well-organized Sagoths advancing at a rapid trot. They wore leather jerkins and kilts and carried ropes and nets in addition to the cudgels and knives at their belts. They sighted us at the same moment and a hoarse cry went up from both sides.

I had no time to organize an attack. The two groups met with a crash. The Sagoths were surprised at the ferocity of the attack and the front rank went down without drawing their weapons. They had probably been informed that a group of gilaks had "escaped," and had been sent to round us up, hardly expecting much resistance. They quickly discovered their error, however, and I saw the leader send one running back the way they had come. Reinforcements would soon be on the way, I had no doubt. Shouting encouragement to my followers, I rushed into the fray. Varna close behind me, one hand on my belt, the other wielding her knife.

At the moment, the carnage and confusion were unbelievable. Fully a dozen Sagoths were down and half as many human beings. The stones of the street were beginning to run with blood. At least, I thought, as I engaged a big Sagoth, the Mahars will be given a day to remember. Except, my mind hastened to confuse me by adding, there are no days in Pellucidar, where it is always noon.

My opponent aimed a mighty blow at me with his weapon, but I countered with my axe and the blade sheared through the shaft of his stone-bladed warclub. A second stroke slammed into his chest and knocked him down. The Sagoths pulled back and re-formed in a group up the street.

"I think we can get through them with one more rush," I cried encouragingly. "Let's catch our breath and then hit them hard."

"Chris, Chris," Varna was tugging at my waist, "look behind. We are surrounded."

I glanced back. The girl was only too right. Another dozen of the ape-men had come out of a side alley and filled the street behind us.

"Ho, Red Axe," called Elkar, "we are now surrounded and outnumbered. The time has come to die or surrender."

"Then we shall die bravely, my friend," I called. "No, wait, there is one more chance! The entrance to this building! Into it, all of you, quickly!"

My little band of gilaks was quick to obey, but as we ran to the open doorway of the building I indicated, a howl arose from our pursuers. Looking back as I reached the entrance, I saw the ape-men running after us. A quick glance, however, showed me a hinged door, propped open, of heavy wood and iron.

"Quick, Varna, we must close this," I gasped. In a moment, we had it shut and latched and I could hear the futile pounding of the Sagoths on the other side.

"That will slow them down," I said, "let us hope there's no easy second entrance." But as we turned back from the door, I found the rest of the escaped prisoners frozen in horror as they regarded the creature now advancing towards us down the passage. It was only a large Mahar and it was unarmed, but the primitive folk were so filled with superstitious fear by the reptiles that not a hand was raised against it. With cold, glittering, snake-like eyes, the winged monster stalked toward me in the dim light of the passageway, and I realized that not one of my companions was going to make a move to aid me.

X

OUT OF THE TRAP

I suppose the Mahar thought it could cow the entire lot of us, walk through us to the door and open it to allow us to be recaptured. Actually, the reptilian creature could not let us invade the building, for reasons we were soon to discover.

The big-eyed, beaked head was as high as my own. The creature opened its toothed mouth menacingly as it approached me. It took one swing, two-handed on the axe handle, to decapitate the monster completely. It fell at my feet, twitching and writhing, the beak opening and closing on the severed head.

My band of ex-slaves gaped at me in disbelief. I stepped over the mobile corpse and proceeded down the passage. When I looked back, I saw several of the cave people poke at the dead Mahar anxiously, and then, with cries of delight, fall upon the body and batter and kick it unmercifully. I could understand their feelings. They had seen fellow human beings devoured by these horrid creatures. Yet, the sight of them wreaking vengeance on the headless body sickened me.

"Come on," I called. "Quickly, everyone, we must seek some new way of escape from this building! Does anyone know where we are? Has anyone been here before?"

No one had. A quick search of the building brought us to a room guarded by four more Mahars. This time the reptiles were quickly dispatched by the armed cave men. Having seen me attack one of the "master-race" and survive, put heart into them.

A glance within the chamber revealed only that it was almost pitch dark. There were no sunlight shafts into the room, only two dim red bulbs on the far wall. At first, I thought it was a storeroom of some sort, for there were regular holes about a foot square dug into all four walls. It was too dark to see what was contained within them. My curiosity was aroused, and I entered the room, feeling my way in the dark.

"Christopher, don't!" hissed Varna. "This is some magic place of the Mahars. There were only Mahars in the building, they must not let the Sagoths in here. It is something evil, come away quickly!"

"No, wait," I said, putting my hand cautiously

into one of the black holes in the wall. Nothing but dry straw. I tried another. This time my hand encountered a round, firm object about the size of a small melon. I picked it up and brought it to the doorway where there was a little more light. The thing was greyish-brown in color and ovoid in shape. The outside was firm but flexible. I was tired from the day's long battle. My mind refused to function. I couldn't imagine what the object might be. Some kind of food, I supposed.

"Sagoths!" called a voice from the door. "Red Axe, Sagoths come!" Cries and the clash of battle came from farther down the corridor. The ape-men must have found another entrance—perhaps some passage to the basement from another building. I could see little of the melee, so I called to my men to fall back. There was a ramp, presumably leading up to the next level, close to where Varna and I stood. The corridor was narrow enough that I thought we could hold it against a siege, particularly if we blockaded it. Unfortunately, at the moment at least, material for a barricade did not seem to be at hand. We retreated to the upward ramp and I absentmindedly carried the object from the storeroom with me as we fell back.

Shortly, I found myself confronting the Sagoths. The front ranks were armed with stone-headed axes in each hand. My gilaks were retreating in good order, but we were losing men, which we could ill afford. I shouted to Varna and those behind me to find something to block the top of the ramp. It looked like we had better do something quickly or we would be all killed off. There was much crashing and shouting behind me as well as in front of me, and then Elkar's voice called that they had a table across the hallway. I cried to those in front of me to run up the ramp and over the obstruction, and three or four of them did so. I was left facing several angry Sagoths while others crowded behind them. Before I withdrew, I threw the round thing in my hand at them. It was really a second thought, I had my axe in my other hand and I didn't want the thing impeding my escape.

It was a bad throw and the thing smashed on the stone wall and its liquid contents dripped down to the floor. In the midst of the clear liquid, however, I could see a four-limbed, big eyed form. It seemed to kick feebly on the floor. The huge Sagoths stopped and stared at it in horror. And then I finally realized what it was.

"Eggs!" I cried, as I jumped over the barricade, "Mahar eggs! Quick, someone see if there is a room of them on this floor, too."

"There are," panted the man next to me, nursing a bruised and broken shoulder. "We got this thing to block the cave-way from a cavern with many holes like the one below."

"You can not fight well with that wound," I said. "Go quickly and bring me more of these eggs. Get the women to help you."

I stood up so my head and shoulders could be seen from below. "Stop, you Sagoths," I called. "Come no farther. We have many of the unborn Mahars at our mercy. We will kill them if you attack."

The man I had sent to the incubator room—I do not know what else to call it—returned and laid four of the ungainly eggs at my feet. There was much rumbling and grumbling among the ape folk below, and then a large Sagoth with a broad leather belt around his waist and a string of skulls around his neck, worked his way to the foot of the slope and looked up at us.

"Stupid gilaks," he called to us, "come down from

143

there and be killed. Masters say kill you all. If you harm the Masters' eggs we will tear you to pieces."

"Stupid ape-man," I retorted, "you will kill us if we come down. Tell your masters we might spare the eggs if one of them will come to talk to us."

"Me not stupid," cried the infuriated beast, and he bounded up the ramp toward me. I threw three of the reptile eggs as he advanced. This time my aim was better and I hit him twice. All three eggs smashed. Then the Sagoth, partly blinded by gooey egg in his eyes, was trying to climb over the up-turned table and get at us. Three cudgel wielding cave men attacked him as he did so and, with cries of baffled rage, he jumped down and ran back to his mates. A cry of triumph went up from my besieged gilaks.

"Mooh-lah, Elkar, search the rest of the building, make sure there are no other ways for them to get in," I hurriedly directed. "The rest of you, find more rocks to strengthen our defense."

I called down again to the Sagoths below, "Go, one of you, and bring some of the masters to talk to us." They hesitated, the big fellow who had charged us arguing with several others. The creatures were so stupid I feared they might never make up their minds.

"We can not escape," I shouted. I hoped that we could, as a matter of fact. "Leave a guard and go to the Great Ones. If we destroy their eggs, they will be very angry and you will feel the weight of that anger."

Apparently, many of the Sagoths agreed with me, for one of their number departed and the rest, under the leadership of their egg-splattered captain, squatted down to wait.

How I wished that I, too, could rest! But first, as a good general, I needed to inspect our defenses.

144

It didn't take long. Our situation was bleak. The building was three stories high and we were trapped on the second floor. There were two small incubator rooms, containing perhaps a hundred eggs, on our floor where we had the access barricaded with various pieces of furniture. The third floor was miscellaneous storage and empty rooms—perhaps the Mahar occupants had lived there. Only on the top floor were there windows, and there several slit-like windows in each room and a huge open skylight in the roof gave access to light and air.

With the help of Mooh-lah, Varna and I clambered up to the roof. Here, for the first time, I had a view of the underground city of the Mahars. For we were still underground. The rough, rocky roof of the cavern loomed twenty feet above our heads. Brilliant shafts of sunlight fell through the openings in that roof to illuminate the strange vistas of the city. One of these openings, and they had to be of considerable size, was almost directly over us, so that the perpetual noon-day sun fell into a broad avenue on our left. The avenue itself was now crowded with Sagoths and slaves staring up at our rooftop. Glancing about, I could see that nearby rooftops were manned with armed Sagoths. No escape there, and the nearest roof was fifty feet away. The low, squat buildings, each carved out of solid stone, stretched away as far as I could see in all directions. Shaft after shaft of sunlight beamed through the dusk and the entire subterranean city had a weird aspect, like a suburb of hell itself. In the distance, I could see winged forms flitting through the gloom—it made the landscape look all the more like Hades.

"Varna," I asked, "are those thipdars?"

She peered in the direction I indicated, but shook her head. "No, I think those are Mahars. They are not large enough for the giant thipdar, and they carry no riders."

"Good," I said. Her eyes were sharper than mine and used to gazing across the vistas of her home mountains . . . Varna's home—would she ever see it again? Looking at our present situation, it seemed unlikely. I drew her to me, and she somehow felt my mood, as she so often did. I held her to my breast with one arm and she placed her slim fingers on my face.

"Fear not, my warrior," she whispered, "you and I will yet leave this gloomy place of death and slavery and stand in the clear sunlight of Pellucidar together."

"Thank you, my darling," I said simply. There is no way to tell such a woman how much she means to you—nor is there any need to, she knows.

We made a quick circle of the rooftop. A low parapet protected the edge. Below us, groups of Sagoths guarded every quarter—no chance of escaping over the side unobserved. At one end of the roof was a square stone box, three feet high, covered with a heavy lid. I levered the lid off and had Mooh-lah lower it to the men below to be used as part of the barricade. Inside, blocks of metal lay in neat rows in an oily liquid which filled the container to the brim.

"Battery," I muttered, "don't touch the fluid, it's acid, it burns. Probably for the lights in the egg rooms." I found a wire cable descending through a hole bored in the stone roof.

"Back down," I decided, "the current's probably too weak to use as a weapon, but the cable may supply us with a rope." I left Mooh-lah and a wounded cave man on the roof to give warning if we were attacked by air. Varna and I went below.

The rebels had found a little food and water in the store rooms and enough straw and containers to build a small fire. They looked battered but cheerful. Our numbers were sadly reduced, however. There were only ten of us left including two other women besides Varna. Elkar was still with us, and the tailed Mooh-lah and, of course, the indomitable Gash.

I located the electric cable running along the ceiling of the passage and cut it with my axe. We pulled it loose and soon had several hundred feet of stiff, insulated wire that looked strong enough to bear a man's weight. Escape off the roof looked impossible, however, as long as the building was guarded. The other useful thing the pillage turned up was a pad of paper and a stylus. I prevented these from being used as fuel for the fire and sat down to write a "ransom note" for the clutch of eggs in our possession.

It was not long after I finished that two Mahars arrived. They stood at the foot of the slope looking up at us, surrounded by a knot of excited Sagoths, some of whom, I was sorry to see, were now armed with spears. They looked important; both had metal neck collars and anklets on, and the big ape-men treated them with considerable respect. We stood behind our makeshift defense of stone tables, rocks, broken pottery and trash, and watched them wave and gesticulate at each other.

Finally, I called down and asked that one of the Sagoths take my written message to the reptiles. When this had been done, there was even more furor and wild flappings of Mahar wings. My demands were simple—we would smash all the eggs unless we were allowed to leave the city unharmed. If this were permitted, we would carry the eggs with us and deliver them to a small party of Sagoths when we reached safety. The problem was, of course, that the conceited creatures didn't believe that I could read and write. The entire thing was, to them, inexplicable, and they could not understand how I had obtained the written message.

Finally, the captain of the Sagoths came part way up the incline and called to me, "The Great Ones say you have one of their number imprisoned in the upper chambers," he said. "You must release him before they will act on your message."

"There is no one up here," I complained. "Let one of them come and see. We will not harm him."

But this they refused to do, and it seemed that we had reached an impasse in the negotiations until I realized what the problem was. "Oh, hell," I told the Sagoth warrior, "they don't believe me. Tell them to get Zed," and I carefully wrote out the symbols of his name. "He can assure them that I am real."

The puzzled Sagoth took the pad to the two Mahars, who studied it a while and then departed. The Sagoths and the humans settled down to glaring at each other, but there was no action.

It seemed an eternity before yelling and confusion on the floor below announced the arrival of a party of Mahars. This time Zed was among them and he mounted the stairwell to the barricade armed with pad and pencil.

The first thing the poor fellow did was write me an essay on the immorality of killing innocent eggs. He seemed actually somewhat emotional about this, although it is difficult for me to judge emotion in these reptiles. He certainly was agitated and jumpy.

Finally, I seized the paper from him and wrote as rapidly as I could: "All of this is beside the
148

point, but we were in danger of death ourselves, yes, and our mates and their unborn eggs as well."

This seemed to slow him down, and he quit flapping his wings and clacked his toothed beak nervously.

I wrote on: "To the point, we are now in control of some dozens of Mahar eggs. We will not harm these if we are allowed to escape ourselves unharmed from the city."

"How do I know you have not already destroyed them?" he wrote.

"Come and see," I wrote in reply.

There was a conference with the Mahars below, and the captain of the Sagoths seemed particularly alarmed by my proposal. Finally, Zed climbed over our defensive barricade, however, and joined me on the other side.

"We decided that I am not important and it does not matter if you slay me," he wrote succinctly.

"I would not slay you, anyway," I wrote back. "Although I would pretend to if it would help. You are one who has been close to me." The Mahar language has, as far as I know, no word for "friend."

When we reached the darkened egg room, several curious cave men following at our heels, Zed went rather quickly to one particular opening and checked its contents. Then he made a rapid tour of the chamber, feeling into each egg cavity with his wing fingers.

"There are four missing," he wrote.

"We threw them at the Sagoths," I replied directly.

He stood motionless for a long minute, and then wrote me a long note, turned and walked out of the room, down the corridor and climbed over the barricade with much flapping of leathery wings.

I read his last message. "This is a desperate situation you are in, Red Axe. I wish you had remained quietly in the laboratory. The ruling twelves may reject your proposal completely. They are enraged that you have killed Mahars and Sagoths and destroyed some unborn. They may feel it more important to make an example of you than to preserve the rest of this clutch of eggs. I will try to persuade them to let you go. I trust you, but I think you have gotten yourself into a trap from which there is no escape. I hope we can prevent further destruction of the eggs. One of them is mine." The message was signed with the strange Mahar characters that represented Zed's name or, actually, his serial number.

I read the incredible message to Varna. She gasped, "Oh, I'm glad his egg did not get smashed. It must be the first one he went to, do you remember . . .?" But neither of us could recall which niche the winged reptile had gone toward.

"It does not matter," I said. "and I think he would do his best for us anyway."

A big Neanderthal came to the door. "The Sagoths are restless," he said.

I went to look. It appeared that they were only "changing the guard," but I was dismayed to see more spears and javelins in evidence. Under the cover of a barrage of missiles, it would be possible for the Sagoths to rush our defenses. I had the men on the roof bring down the stone vat of acid for the storage battery and set it behind the barricade so we could pour it down the stone incline. I could think of little else to do. We rested.

It wasn't long before Zed was back. The ungainly creature hopped over the barricade, a pad of paper in one wing hand and a stylus in the other. He came quickly to the point.

"I am to offer you free, safe conduct to the city's

gates if you leave all the eggs here unharmed," he wrote.

"We would be stupid to do that," I replied. "We will take as many of them with us as we can carry and release them only when we get to the edge of the open plain that surrounds the city."

"I am to persuade you to leave without any eggs, and to walk out carrying only your weapons."

"And then what will happen to us?" I asked.

He wrote for a moment and then handed me the pad. "Outside the building, a large number of Sagoths will fall upon you and tear you to pieces."

I stared at him a moment in astonishment. The large eyes in the bird-like head regarded me silently, first one and then the other as the creature turned his head from side to side to look at me.

"Why do you tell me this?" I wrote.

"I do not agree with this decision. Like you, I sometimes make up my mind for myself."

There was no way to show my feelings. If he had been a man, I would have embraced him, or at least clasped his hand. With this winged dinosaur, I had no idea how to respond. I wrote, "I am grateful."

"It is fair," he wrote back, "that you know the alternatives. You are a reasoning being." Coming from one of the master race of the inner world, that was a compliment indeed. "What do you intend to do now?" Zed asked.

"If I can not think of a way to escape," I wrote, "we will let you fly off from the roof with your egg. We will cast the rest of the eggs off the roof, set fire to anything that will burn, hurl the acid vat into the Sagoths below, and charge into them until we are all killed."

I read the correspondence aloud to Varna and the others while Zed pondered. The Sagoths below became restless again. They could see the Mahar's head above the barricade, but they called up, saying he must return.

"There must be some better plan, Red Axe," said Elkar.

Zed wrote a quick note and handed it to me. It said, "There must be some better plan."

"Zed," I wrote, "can you carry us, one at a time. and fly to the ventilation holes in the roof?"

"No," he wrote, and then on another page, "Impossible. Try to lift my body."

I did as he suggested. The scaly hide was dry and even warm. Placing both hands on his torso, I could easily lift him up at arm's length. The winged body was as big as a man's and even with the wings folded looked large, but the creature's bones must be hollow and the slender body contain only skeleton and vital organs. He could not have weighed more than a hundred pounds. There was no way that fragile, kite-like frame could lift the weight of a human being. The powerful thipdars were larger, heavier and had a gigantic wing span, which was probably why we did not see them inside the underground city.

"Wait," I cried, "I do have a plan!" I called to the Sagoths that we were coming down, grabbed the coil of electric cable and beckoned Zed to accompany me. We ran to the roof opening and scrambled out. Mooh-lah was on duty. "Quick," I directed the tailed man, "tie some knots in the length of this."

"Zed," I wrote, "can you carry one end of this rope out through the roof and fasten it?" I pointed up at the vent above our heads, twenty or thirty feet away. In answer, he seized the heavier end of the cable in his feet, spread his bat-like wings and with much flapping, took to the air. A moment later,

I saw him enter the shaft of sunlight and disappear through the hole in the cavern roof above us.

A cry from below, "Red Axe, the Sagoths attack!"

"Throw the acid and retreat up here," I shouted. Above our heads, a flying figure reappeared, circled once and then exited again. I pulled on the cable, it looked slender and weak all that long distance. My troops tumbled out onto the roof top behind me.

Now I was faced with a new problem. Should I lead my group into the unknown or stay behind and cover the retreat? Varna solved the problem for me very neatly. She looked at the long wire dangling from the roof of the cave and shook her head.

"I do not trust Mahars that much," she said, "he may well have set a new trap for us on the surface, or intend to drop us all to the ground once we're on the rope. Christopher, you will have to lead, if you expect any of us to follow."

Indeed, it did look thin and precarious as I started up. The others held the wire below, but it still swayed violently with each movement of my body. I looked down briefly, but the dizzying height and the effect produced by my twisting and turning around as I ascended made me nauseous and I concentrated on watching the cable directly under my hands, and working as fast as I could. Mooh-lah had managed to space a few knots in the cable, and these enabled me to rest and catch my breath. I still did not look down. There were a few violent jerks on the strand below me and then, after what seemed an eternity of climbing, my shoulder struck the rough-hewn rock of the cavern roof. I had a bad moment getting past the point where the wire cable lay tight against the rock.

The going beyond that point, however, was easy,

because the shaft itself had been man-made and there were hand holds and climbing bars left by the workmen. To one of these, Zed had tied the end of the cable.

Below me a voice cried, "Christopher!" and I reached down to pull Varna to a spot beside me on the rock. The trip up the rope had not fazed her in the least and she soon caught her breath. "The Sagoths pursue us," she said, "but Mooh-lah released the tail of the rope, so there are only two on it and it swings free."

Zed descended from above, flapping to a perch near us as the rest of my party began to arrive. Mooh-lah was last, and he leaped to safety with a cry, "Sagoths below, Red Axe! Cut the rope!"

I pulled my axe from my belt, where I had hung it during my climb. As I swung to sever the wire cable, the big, hairy hand of one of the pursuing Sagoths appeared around the lip of the shaft. As the cable parted, he hung for just a moment and then, with a cry, he fell.

The rocky shaft was over ten feet deep, but the sturdy cave folk clambered easily to the top. Brilliant sunlight blinded us as we reached the rim. Bright green grass stretched away in all directions. To our right, the top of one of the guard towers could be seen and as we crawled out onto the plain, the rest of the tower came into view.

Our troubles were far from over. Out of a gate at the base of the tower emerged a party of armed Sagoths, headed in our direction. I glanced about. Only a few hundred yards to the left, the ground sloped down to the edge of a green and inviting woods. Under these trees, we would be safe from the eyes of flying thipdars and perhaps lose the pursuing Sagoths.

"Come on!" I cried, seizing Varna by the hand and leading the run across the close cropped grass of Phuma toward the inviting cover of the forest. Zed took wing as we ran, circling over us and rapidly gaining altitude.

XI

THE ENDLESS SWAMP

We put our pursuers to our heels and raced for the forest. Zed spiraled up above us and out of sight. My worst fear was the great winged thipdars. Until we were under the trees, we could still be picked off by the monster pterodactyls. Fortunately, our escape through the roof had been fast enough and unexpected enough that an effective pursuit was not immediately started. When we reached the cover of the trees and relative safety from aerial attack and surveillance, the Sagoths were still far to our rear, shouting and cursing.

I slowed my pace slightly but kept the group moving among the trees, which were here widely spaced and not large. My eyes had adjusted to the sunlight but not yet to the brilliant colors of Pellucidar. Behind us was the lush green meadow and the stone guard towers of the plain of Phuma. Beyond, the forest began again and in the distance, I could see the gleam of a river among the trees. Beyond that, the greenery went on and on until it faded into the haze and the bright sunshine. Close ahead, the treetops loomed, covered with vines, to block the view, but beyond them was only an impression of endless, ever-changing shades of green. Pellucidar, being the inside of a hollow ball, has no horizon.

Varna caught my hand. "Which way, Chris?" she cried. She, too, I could see, was intoxicated by the sunlight and the greenery. How could I have kept her with me in that grey underground world all these months?

"The Sagoths will pursue, I'm sure," I said.

"They are said to be excellent trackers," she said, "and they know the country."

"Which way is the land of Val-an?" I asked her. Without hesitation she pointed ahead and slightly to our left. Once again I was amazed at the strange ability of the people of Pellucidar to find direction without sun movements, moon or stars to guide them. Obviously in a land of perpetual noon, they needed some sort of homing instinct or they would be continuously lost, but how did it work? A research problem for another time, I decided.

"Good," I told her. "We will all run in that direction until we can put some miles between us and the Sagoths."

Tall grew the trees around us as we ran. Sometimes there were vague game trails, other times we forced our way through thick undergrowth that clung to our bodies with stubborn branches, making every step a struggle.

Huge dragonflies buzzed around us and flocks of birds, disturbed by our advance, rose up from the ground cover to roost in the trees. Some of them scolded noisily as we passed, as did a chattering troop of monkeys we surprised in a banana grove. They took to the tree tops, screaming their indignation as we stripped the ripe bananas from the lower branches. Eating, we hurried on under the great vine-covered arches of the jungle that rose before us. I hoped the noise of the disturbed monkeys would not draw our Sagoth pursuers. Always I followed Varna's direction. At least I knew we were in no danger of circling aimlessly, the common fate of the surface dweller, enclosed as we were in forest and out of sight of terrestrial landmarks.

Our flight led us to what seemed to be the rim of a great valley and as we pushed downhill, climbing over and around the huge roots of the trees whose foliage now blotted out much of the sunlight, I could hear the plunging and crashing of large animals far ahead of us.

"Mooh-lah," I asked the tailed man who loped along beside me at the moment, "what do you make of that?"

He listened for a moment. "Big," he commented, "but no squealing. Probably not tantor (the mamoth), perhaps some other tuskers, their relatives."

"Dangerous?"

"Usually not. Sometimes an old buck or a cow with young, they think you attack, then they charge. Usually they just move aside, you walk past."

And so it happened. We came upon the first group of the beasts suddenly. The huge grey shapes seemed all around us. Some of them must have been fifteen feet tall and they looked as big as houses. They had small ears and rudimentary trunks, but as Mooh-lah said, they looked like relatives of the elephant or the mastodon. They were hairless and their underjaws were overgrown into huge, toothed shovels. They had been rooting up the soggy earth like a herd of pigs, and they stopped as we approached.

"Move slow and don't talk," whispered Mooh-lah. "Do not move suddenly, do not walk right at them or they misunderstand." He began to sing in a low, clear voice, singing to the huge beasts around us.

"Now, now, my little ones. Do not fear us, my children. See, we move softly over the ground. Now, now, all is well, my little ones."

We threaded our way, walking slowly so as not to make any sudden move, single file, among the great hulks. Some continued to watch us, others, lulled perhaps by the half-man's singing, turned back to chomping on the thick green rushes that grew in the soft, muddy earth.

I led the way, watching one big bull whose pig-like ears were twitching wildly as we passed close in front of him. Was he wiggling his ears like that because he disliked us, or merely to keep off the flies? The soft mud clung to my feet and I sank into it again and up to my knees. If the beast were to charge me, I could never have run, anyway.

In single file we passed the first group of grazing beasts only to encounter another family of them a little farther on. There was no point now in turning back and trying to go around their feeding ground, the group behind us might become excited at our return. On we went, literally under the noses of the great elephantine creatures. They sniffed and snorted uneasily, and several of them moved warily off into the jungle.

Mooh-lah kept right on singing to them, "Ah, there are many of my brothers. Many of my brothers feed today. Is the food good, my little ones? Ah, do not gnash your teeth and glare at me. I am small and you are the mighty ones. Mighty ones, do not bother the little folk who run between their legs." On and on he went, improvising and then repeating himself over and over. It was rather hypnotic, I thought, as I picked my way (slowly, not too fast) over a mass of fallen trees and saw yet another group of beasts ahead of us, but farther off to the left. Then I noticed that Varna had the giggles. I tried to catch her eye and frown at her to get her to stop. She avoided my gaze, however, and choked her amusement behind her hand.

Whether it was luck, or Mooh-lah's serenade, we made it through the marshy ground without being charged by a shovel-toothed pseudo-mastodon. I, for one, was relieved to climb up a slope beyond among thicker trees that offered some protection from the great creatures. Clusters of purple flowered orchids hung from the trees and the ground was covered with fresh and rotting tree branches. We found perches among the boughs and sat down to rest.

We were a bedraggled-looking lot. There were three women, counting Varna, and seven men. All of us, the women included, had minor wounds from our battles with the Sagoths. Our skins were covered with a mixture of dried blood, mud from the marsh we had just passed, green juices from the plants and grasses we had been forcing our way through for hours, and sweat. None of us had much left in the way of clothing, it had been torn off in our wild flight through the jungle. We were exhausted. I suggested that we rest a while before proceeding further.

While I was talking, there was a flapping of wings above our heads. "Thipdar!" cried one of the men, and we all ducked and looked for cover. A quick glance upward, however, revealed a much smaller form flapping to a perch just above us. It was Zed!

I stared at him in amazement. He regarded me quietly with his deep eyes, using the Mahar trick of turning the head from side to side so that the image falls first on one retina, then the other.

"He is here to kill us!" someone hissed. I heard a rustle of weapons.

"No, wait," I said, "if he wanted to kill us, all

he had to do was not fasten the rope by which we escaped from the city of the Mahars. Let us trust him. We have every reason to trust him, for without him none of us would have escaped."

"How can you be sure it is the same Mahar," a voice grunted.

"Fear not, I know him well. It is the one who helped us before," I replied. But how were the reptile and I to communicate? We humans now had no implements except a few clubs and knives and my own axe. Yet for me to talk to the creature, we must be able to write. I gazed above the tree-filled marsh in perplexity. Varna gave a little cry, jumped off her seat on the branch near me and ran to a nearby bush. In a moment she returned with the broad fleshy leaves of a plant.

"See, Chris," she said, drawing her fingernail along a leaf, "writing!" Indeed, her finger left a dark green bruise on the leaf; a primitive slate-board, but sufficient. I moved closer to the Mahar and wrote on a leaf.

"Sagoths."

"Not near but coming." The creature gestured with an extended wing back toward the beast-filled marsh we had just negotiated.

"Yourself?"

"No return. Death for me in Phuma." I stared at him in momentary disbelief. But really, was it so strange? He was surely a traitor to his own city, to his own species.

"I sorrow," I wrote. I meant it, too.

"Decision necessary," he wrote. "Help you, then I must face death from Mahars." He ran out of leaf paper and Varna and I went to gather more. "However," he continued, "it is a balance." (Maybe he meant it was fair or just). "I am only one of my race who could understand you enough to believe you should survive. To me comes a chance to save."

We had run out of leaves again. Zed was writing with a wing claw, fairly small, but only a few characters could be placed on a leaf, and sometimes I had to guess at those.

I would have liked to continue this conversation, or rather correspondence, for in it I began to see some Mahar philosophy. Maybe it was Zed's personal philosophy, but that was one of the things I wanted to explore. For now, however, there were more immediate considerations. My little army of rebels was restless. The presence of one of the enemy upset them no matter what I could say.

My leadership of the group had remained unquestioned as long as the escape was in progress. Now that we had reached freedom, I felt my control on the diverse group of cave men dissolving. Nor was there any reason why I should try to maintain it.

I ascertained from Zed in which direction the Sagoth pursuit lay. I repeated this to the rest. I had been reading them what the Mahar wrote as we went along.

"How many?" I asked.

"Twelve of twelves," Zed wrote. There was a gasp from my audience when I repeated this figure.

"We had better all get moving," I said. "I had hoped we could rest a while here, but the Sagoths seem determined to kill us or drag us back to slavery in Phuma. Now, I think it would be better if we went in several directions. If they are so many, we will never be able to fight them. Let each man now return to his own tribe. What do you say?"

"Good," grunted one of the heavyset cave men. "We go."

"The Sagoths lie behind us," I gestured back

161

across the thick marsh where the big elephant creatures could still be heard rooting and chomping. "Our way lies—Varna, which way do we go?" She pointed off into the surrounding jungle without hesitation.

"My tribe's hunting grounds are somewhere there also," said Mooh-lah. He was perched higher up in the fallen tree branches than the rest of us, his tail wrapped around a convenient limb. He looked off in the direction of "home," and sighed. "A long way, but I will go."

"Good, you will go with us, then." I was genuinely glad to have his company. His knowledge of the jungle might be lifesaving. Elkar and I had no experience in such surroundings and Varna knew only the wild life of her own mountains.

"Elkar," I said, turning to the pale albino-faced city dweller, "all this must seem strange to you."

He grinned bravely. "Strange indeed, Red Axe. A world full of huge trees," he gestured, "and strange unnameable beasts. And now I am the only one here who has no tribe to go to."

"Not so, my friend," I hastened to assure him. "Our tribe, Varna's tribe, can offer you a home. Varna, do you think the Val-an would adopt him as they did me?"

"To be sure, Red Axe," she laughed, "and for such a man, tall, strong, good looking, the girls of Val-an would be most happy to make room among their sleeping furs!" Elkar had the good manners to blush.

I laughed at him. "Then you come with us also!" I said. "That's too good an invitation to refuse!"

"I will accompany you, at least as far as the land of the ferocious Had-bar," said a new voice. Gash, of course, Gash the indestructible. I merely grunted. There was no point in pretending I wanted his company, but he had been of help. Also, it was not his fault the first escape attempt had failed.

The other five went off in different directions. Two of them had to circle back towards the Mahar city, a risky business at best. I asked Zed again where the pursuing Sagoths were, and we sent the pair—they were mates—off at an angle to avoid contact with them. The other three decided to set off together in yet another direction. This left me with only one major problem—the Mahar.

I took a "note-leaf" and wrote him briefly. "We must go, and hurry. Come with my group. You can fly ahead, seeing the direction we are going, and meet me when we stop to rest."

I watched him intently as he turned the message over in his claws. I was anxious to have the creature accept my invitation, although I knew my fellow humans would be less than delighted. I could see great advantages in having an aerial reconnaissance patrol ahead of us in this formidable country.

Zed looked at me a long moment with one eye, and then drew the symbol "yes" in the air with a claw.

We parted from the other rebel slaves with many assurances of friendship and mutual admiration. Within minutes, though, they had vanished silently into the thick jungle overgrowth. I turned to lead our new trek into the unknown. Zed watched us depart, and then took to the air over our heads with a few flaps of his bat-like wings. In a moment he was above the tree tops, and then he, too, was out of sight.

The ground got wetter and the greenery thicker as we went on. There were puddles and little slow streams in the mud, so that we had plenty to drink. Mooh-lah found a few fruits and some edible fern shoots. The ferns were magnificent. They stood ten to twenty feet tall, and the fronds were over six feet wide. Traveling through the thick fern jungle was slow, hot work under the noon-day sun. We had to wander from our intended path to get around impenetrable tangles of undergrowth or the roots of the gigantic trees.

The jungle was crawling with life. Huge insects buzzed hungrily around our heads. Gigantic multi-colored butterflies rose up from the reeds as we passed, some of them with wings as big as my hands, flashing iridescent blues, greens and purples. There were birds, including a flock of multi-colored cockatoos that hooted and screeched at our presence as if they were having their long, decorative tail feathers pulled out one by one. I didn't see any more monkeys, but there were little rodent creatures in the trees, usually moving so fast you couldn't make them out. Almost all of the creatures were species totally unknown to me.

Most amazing of all were the lizards. There were little ones, of course, chameleons among the ferns and grasses, and little tree lizards in the branches. But, in addition, there were great big fellows, up to four feet long, counting their tapering tails. Sometimes we would come upon them suddenly and, startled, they would poise motionless a moment before flashing out of sight among the ferns and bushes. Most of them were shiny-scaled, banded dark and light, although a few were grey or grey-green in color. Some had elaborate ruffs and dorsal spines or fins like iguanas. The giant monitor lizards of Komodo, I knew, grew to be eight or more feet long. Some of these fellows could be that big, but so far none of them offered us any harm. Just as I was musing that I had never seen such a variety of reptilian life, although no snakes as yet,

I climbed over a mass of broken tree ferns and came upon an even more amazing sight.

There were a horde of the little creatures feeding among the grasses. At my arrival, they scampered in all directions. These, too, were lizard-like, but they had long, swaying necks as well as long, scaly tails, and they ran erect on their hind legs like ridiculous chickens. Their tiny forelegs, with which they had been grubbing in the soil, were held up in front of them as they ran. the long tails held straight out behind to balance their bodies. In a flash, they were gone. Mooh-lah had come up quietly behind me.

"More dyryths, little dyryths," he said. "Good eating."

"Good," I said, "I am hungry. Let's capture some." But although we spread out and tried to encircle them, the diminutive, ostrich-like creatures were too quick and wily for us. They dashed between us while we flailed at the empty air and they scuttled off. Eventually, we settled for a larger, slow-moving monitor-like lizard about four feet long. Elkar speared him with a sharpened stick and the rest of us finished him off with knives and hatchets.

Varna managed to start a fire, using dried moss and bits of tree fern, and we roasted slices of the lizard's tail over the flames. I've eaten iguana in Mexico and it is palatable. This prehistoric reptile was probably no better, but I was starving, and the half-cooked meat was delicious.

Zed located our cook fire and flew down through the tree tops and giant ferns to join us. Unlike the humans, however, he preferred his meat raw. Watching him tear at the lizard's carcass with his great toothed beak reminded me of the ghastly scene in the sacrificial lake. I wondered if Zed, too, had eaten live human beings? Probably he had, and would again, if the opportunity arose.

When we had finished, I carefully buried the fire, although Mooh-lah assured me that the Sagoths would have little trouble following the trail we had left.

"Our best hope is to keep ahead of them," he said, "and to take to the trees, where trails are hard to follow."

"I will do as you suggest," I said, "but first we must rest."

I thought we might camp out on the ground if we could find any reasonably dry ground to do it on, but my companions insisted that it was unsafe to be anywhere but in the trees.

I yielded to their experience, and we climbed into a forest giant not far from where we had eaten. I cut a few limbs with my axe, and with creepers we tied together a platform across several branches some thirty feet above the ground. I arranged for one man to stay awake. The great Mahar perched near us, and, as far as I knew, he required no sleep, but I did not trust him alone to keep watch.

I lay down with Varna at my side, my axe close to my hand. I was exhausted. The jungle was full of noises—the creak of tree limbs, the buzz of insects, the sigh of the wind in the higher foliage, the chatter of birds, the slithering of some large, reptilian beast in the undergrowth. I was wondering how I could ever ignore it all and relax, when I fell asleep.

It was, of course, still noon when we awoke. Mooh-lah had gathered a handful of fruit and we shared this among us. Varna and I found a cool, shaded pool and we bathed. Elkar joined us, but Gash and the monkey-tailed Mooh-lah disdained the idea of getting wet.

When we set out on our journey again, it was through the treetops. Mooh-lah led the way, his tail curled up over his shoulder except when he used it to hold on. Varna followed him, light-footed and agile, to keep us going in the right direction. Elkar and I were behind, being the least experienced climbers, and Gash brought up the rear, grumbling and complaining. Zed would join us for a while and then wing away over the treetops to wait for us farther on. The whole operation was far from noise-less. Varna assured me, however, that tree snakes and other vermin would move out of our way if they heard us coming. "And if any creature wants to stalk us, five of us can not move quietly enough to prevent it."

I had agreed, reluctantly, to taking to the trees, because I thought it would slow us down. To my surprise, the going was easier and faster than it had been on the marshy ground. For one thing, the limbs of many of the jungle giants were broad thorough-fares, without the slightest danger of falling. We wandered along boughs that stretched out hundreds of feet, bordered and entwined with flowering vines and orchids.

A hundred feet above the ground, we meandered across limbs that must have been twenty feet thick. At times, we strayed from our original orientation, but Varna kept us going in the general direction of Val-an, and we crossed from limb to limb of the forest giants on thick bridges of vines. Only rarely did we have to descend from one tree in order to ascend another. Most of the great trees were so in-tertwined with their neighbors that one stepped from the broad boughs of one to the other, hardly breaking stride.

There were several other advantages to using the upper levels of the forest for locomotion. It was cooler than the humid, stagnant air at ground level. Breaks in the unending roof of foliage brought gusts of fresh air as well as beams of welcome sunlight into the green gloom. Also, the animals were smaller. We were still surrounded by an unending variety of insect and lizard life. Occasionally, we saw small birds and arboreal mammals, but all of these creatures were of smaller size than those we had encountered on the ground. I kept a close watch to either side, however, for Varna warned me that leopards and other great cats made their lairs in the upper levels of the great trees. If we disturbed them, however, they must have been well-fed and slunk off unseen.

Varna stopped me where a break in the leaves gave us a window out of the trees to the ground below. The grasses and ferns were swaying with the passage of some great beasts, and occasionally, I could see a great, grey back heave up into sight.

"Elephants (tantor)?" I whispered.

"No," she answered, sniffing the air with her dainty nose. "Some kind of gryf." We could hear the creatures snorting and stomping in the undergrowth, but could not get any better glimpse of them.

We set out again along the branches, occasionally actually swinging from one forest path to another on loops of vines. A strange procession we made. Our leader, the monkey-man, running ahead, climbing to the tops of vertical branches with prehensile feet and tail to spy out the way; behind him, the lovely Varna, her long, black hair tied back with a strip of bark and decked with flowers. Clad only in a skimpy loincloth, bare breasted, she wore about her waist a coil of vine from which hung a stone knife and stone-headed axe. Behind her I trudged, dressed much the same as she, barefooted, blond, bearded, with a vine rope and my red bladed axe slung over my back for easy climbing. I think I was less out of place than Elkar, however. The big, pale-haired city man had never been anywhere outside of underground Phuma, and every flower, every bird and insect was a revelation to him. Varna and I had to be constantly stopping to urge him on as he paused to gaze at some new wonder. Gash, dark, beetle-browed and hairy, looked almost as at home in the tree tops as Mooh-lah, but he sullenly refused to join in our gaiety. Varna teased and pelted him with soft, red berries which Mooh-lah had found for us to eat, but he only glared at her.

We had gone thus for miles when Mooh-lah drew us to a halt. He had me climb up above the level we had been traveling. There was a view out of the great tree we occupied. Ahead of us was an area of thick reed and fern and then a stretch of bare water. In the distance, I could see numerous green islands.

"The sea?" I asked.

"No, no, big lake—swamp," he replied. "Can not see how big."

Varna climbed up beside us and seated herself on a limb.

"Which way?" I asked her, and she pointed straight ahead. The landscape tipped up, as Pellucidarian landscape always does, and I thought I could see solid greenery in the distance, but there was mist on the water and I couldn't be sure. To either side, the jungle stretched away and back as far as I could see.

"Perhaps we could raft across it," I suggested, looking down at the water for crocodiles. Then it happened! At first I thought I was witnessing some sort of volcanic eruption and a mountain was rising out of the water only a hundred yards away. But the movement was silent, except for trickles of water running off the sides of the thing. Then I saw that it was big, but not that big. And, as we watched, the long, serpentine neck came up out of the water and towered dozens of feet above the surface. Small, reptilian eyes carefully scanned the shore. The behemoth did not turn but strode directly towards us and now, as it reached the shallows, I could see that it was supported by four massive legs like tree trunks. With an ungainly grumble, it heaved itself ashore, and as the gigantic beast passed directly beneath our tree, I could distinctly feel the branches tremble with each step of its enormous feet.

XII

LAND OF MONSTERS

Scarcely had the first beast passed out of sight among the foliage than a second snake-like neck reared into view. As we watched in awe and amazement, more than a dozen lumbering giants floundered up out of the water of the swamp to browse among the trees. The heads of the creatures were tiny in comparison with their bodies, and the little mouths seemed always full, working as hard as possible to fill those huge stomachs.

"Brontosaurus," I said, staring at them in amazement, "or maybe they're Diplodocus."

"Lidi," said Mooh-lah. "I have never seen such animals, but I have heard of them."

"Are they dangerous?" whispered Varna. "With those long necks they may be able to reach up here in the trees." Indeed, even as she spoke, a coil of neck, topped by a tiny, stupid-looking head, broke through the treetops below us. The great dinosaur did not seem to notice us, however, and fell to browsing on the uppermost sprouts of the giant tree ferns.

"They are plant-eaters, as far as I know," I replied.

Mooh-lah nodded his head vigorously. "They are said to be harmless except when they step upon you unawares. In some far countries, men train them and ride on their backs."

I doubted that, although I would surely like to see it.

"The thing I fear, Red Axe," continued the monkey-man, coiling his tail about a nearby branch, "is that if there is so much meat, there must be meat-eaters nearby."

"I agree," I said, "and from what I remember of the natural enemies of these big fellows, nothing is safe from them."

Several branches above us the leaves shook and there was a flapping of wings. We glanced up in alarm to discover Zed, gripping a branch with both feet; he peered down at us quizzically. Below us, another saurian heaved his bulk and long neck up through the green roof of the jungle to gaze mildly in our direction before returning to his endless grazing.

The branches made a kind of "window" two hundred feet above the ground, and, here, with the herd of great brontosaurs browsing contentedly, we held a council of war. The bright noonday sun gleamed off the waters of the swamp or lake before us. Occasionally, the surface would be disturbed by the movement of some creature beneath, but nothing showed itself.

"I had considered making rafts," I said, "and poling ourselves to the opposite shore. But after seeing the size of the inhabitants of the swamp——"

"No," said Elkar, "I would never risk myself out of the trees near anything so big, even if you and Mooh-lah say they don't eat meat."

"Ah," cried Mooh-lah, "there are plenty of water-dryths that do eat meat, never fear. Look, look there!" and he pointed out across the water. Near one of the marshy islands a great beaked head broke the surface for a moment, blew a cloud of spray and resubmerged. No, I did not care to venture those waters on a log raft.

I had Varna and Mooh-lah scan the upcurving distance and, with gestures and a few Mahar characters cut into the bark with a stone knife, I got Zed to make a reconnaissance flight for us. This turned out to be useful, for he returned and drew us a crude map. The watery part of the swamp was roughly oval and had no long indenting arms. If we set out to circle it we would not have to cut back. I assumed we would still be pursued, there was no point in turning back into the Sagoths' arms. Varna and the monkey-man were sure they could see solid shore on the far side of the swamp. They wouldn't have been able to do so if we had been on the outer surface, the horizon would have cut it off. But here, the land curved up until it was lost in the blue distance, and so continued completely around over our heads—a strange sensation indeed!

My two sharp-eyed observers could not see the extent of the swamp to the left and right of us, but Zed's crude map, scratched in the tree bark with his claws, assured us that there was a limit to it. We were too buried in the greenery of the towering trees to see far in any direction but straight ahead.

Val-an, Varna assured me, lay almost straight ahead.

"We will have to walk around, and I hope the forest holds out, for the ground seems to be inhabited by monsters," I said. "Mooh-lah, where lies your country?"

"My people are there," he replied, pointing with one arm.

"Slightly to the right, anyway," I said, "O.K., we will try to circle the swamp in that direction. First, let's rest a bit. Mooh-lah, do you think you could find us something to eat?"

He grinned. "In this jungle, Red Axe? Meat is so plentiful on the lower levels, my only problem will be to be sure it does not eat me!" He went crashing off through the branches, swinging by his hands and tail indiscriminantly. The rest of us settled down to watching the behemoths grazing on the treetops below us. We were plenty high enough to be above their reach and they seemed to ignore us completely.

Mooh-lah was soon back with two squirrel like creatures tied up in vines. We built a fire on a broad tree branch and roasted them, caught a few hours of sleep and then prepared to continue on our way.

"Look!" cried Elkar, pointing down the shore. Sure enough, something was moving through the tree ferns and undergrowth, moving more rapidly than a browsing brontosaurus, but still with an indefinable air of stealth.

As we watched, several of the great saurians beneath us became alerted. The tiny heads went up on the long necks as they scanned the jungle. Perhaps they smelled something suspicious. Some of the more anxious began to move restlessly, crushing small trees and undergrowth under their giant feet, working their way back toward the water. Too late, for one of them.

With a fearful roar the enemy leaped from his ambush into the herd. In three gigantic bounds he closed with one of the brontosaurs. Although smaller than his prey, he towered fifty feet above the ground on gigantic, muscular hind legs. The tiny forelimbs, although taloned, looked feeble in comparison with the rest of the huge green body and lashing, twenty foot tail. The fanged head alone must have weighed over a ton.

With a shock we could hear in our treetop, the predator hit the feebly running gray green bulk of the fleeing dinosaur. The force of the blow knocked the poor creature completely over. In an instant, his nemesis was upon him. The giant fangs gouged, the huge rear foot talons clawed at the soft underbelly. The long neck of the brontosaurus was arched up and it let out a pitiful wail of pain. The other giants crashed off through the undergrowth or into the water, leaving trails of smashed vegetation behind them.

I realized that I was seeing a drama no man of the outer crust could more than imagine. The attack of the Tyrannosaurus Rex, the biggest, most powerful carnivore in the history of the world. The spectacle held us all spellbound. The brontosaurus was far from defeated. It regained its feet, rending the air with hideous squeals, intermingled now with the snarling of its attacker. The big vegetarian made a valiant rush for the water, but the tyrannosaurus threw itself against the big fellow's shoulders, biting with that gigantic fanged maw into the muscles. The brontosaurus must have had a tough protective hide, for it resisted the first attacks, although the force of the onslaught turned it from its rush to escape and brought it to its knees. The mighty engine of destruction astride its back ripped into the hide and muscles, rending off huge chunks of bleeding flesh.

The brontosaurus lashed with its great tail in futile fashion. Snarling, the tyrannosaurus clung to its shoulders, tearing with its fangs and clawing with its powerful hindquarters. Over and over they rolled on the ground, now almost completely hidden by the grasses and tree ferns, now briefly revealed in agonized, crimson combat. The snarls and screams of predator and prey were mingled with the crashing of falling fern trunks and the splashing and wallowing of the rest of the herd of brontosaurs. Some of these, deep in the water, gazed at the half-hidden battle in mild reproof.

The brontosaurus managed to throw off its attacker. Battered and bleeding, it staggered to its feet and turned to run. The giant carnivore was after him in three strides, but this time was struck a mighty blow by the great flailing tail. The tyrannosaurus was bowled over, hitting the ground with a thud. For a moment it lay stunned, then leaped to its feet again with a roar of fury. A few mighty bounds of those powerful hind legs let the ferocious creature catch up to its prey. Now it evaded the swinging tail, leaped full upon the back of the great gray saurian, driving it to its knees. Up came the long neck of the brontosaurus as it squealed in pain and fear. Down went the great fanged head of the tyrant lizard, great jaws tearing and rending. Its fearful snarls mingled with the death cries of its victim, for those terrible teeth reached vital organs and the great brontosaurus fell into the crushed reeds and ferns at the edge of the swamp. The vitality did not go out of the giant body, however, for even as the tyrannosaurus tore strips of bleeding flesh from the carcass, the tail and legs continued to twitch and writhe.

For a long while we sat stunned by the incredible spectacle. Varna gradually relaxed the grip she had held on my arm. Her fingernails had deeply indented the skin.

No one of my own world has ever witnessed such a fantastic demonstration of reptilian destructiveness. Only some faint racial memory of such beasts keeps alive the myths of dragons and monsters in the mind of modern man. But here, in the lost world of Pellucidar, they still exist!

Gash grunted, pointing to the sky. Dozens of circling winged forms had appeared. "Little flying devils come to feed," he grunted.

"And some not so little," agreed Mooh-lah, "Red Axe, this tree is too close. Soon full of flying meat-eaters. We go now." I nodded, turning with strange reluctance from the scene of death beneath us.

"Lead on, then," I said.

In many places the great trees overhung the waters of the swamp. There was no solid ground beneath us now, only a mass of tree roots and rotting vegetation. Higher among the branches, however, the sun still shone and the leaves were bright. We continued on our way without difficulty. Often the leafy boughs were so entangled with green vines that they formed a flat swaying surface. Other places we climbed laboriously from limb to limb, Mooh-lah plunging ahead of the group, leaping to higher levels and returning with a crash to guide us into the next forest giant. We were making our way along a vine and moss-encrusted path when there was an ominous creaking and swaying of the bough beneath our feet.

"Beware! Dead branch!" cried Mooh-lah, bounding up into a mass of greenery overhead. Before I could move, the footing beneath me gave way. I started to fall, clutched out wildly and felt the monkey-man's prehensile tail coil around my wrist. My arm was nearly jerked from its shoulder-socket and I found myself suspended above an astonishing hole in the forest tapestry, through which I could see the branch fall, crashing again and again into the branches below.

"Oh-oh, a lucky one for you," said Mooh-lah as he dragged me up to the safety of a higher level. We then had to circle back to rejoin our companions, whom we found still on the end of that rent in the arboreal highway. Varna had been behind me, but far enough back to be out of danger.

Mooh-lah rubbed the base of his tail ruefully and complained. "Ah, Red Axe, you much too heavy for me to make a tail catch like that. Nearly pull poor Mooh-lah's tail right off!"

"Nevertheless," I said, "I'm much grateful for that tail, and for your quick action. I was falling before I knew what was happening."

"Yes," he agreed, grinning at me, "you pretty slow, Red Axe. When you start to feel a branch go, you must jump. But I think we have the she walk behind me now. If Mooh-lah have to catch one of you big heavy bucks again, his tail will never be the same!"

It was many hours before I regained my confidence in the treetop paths. I had been blundering along, forgetting that we were trooping through the branches hundreds of feet above the ground. Now the sight of the falling log plunging through the air beneath me kept recurring every time I felt the slightest swaying beneath my feet. I got over my case of nerves with time. I had to, there was nothing to do but keep climbing with the rest of them.

I could hardly insist that we all descend to the ground. Besides, the ground level was probably pitch black under this jungle. With time, my nervousness decreased but I still tended to jump each time a twig cracked. I noticed that Mooh-lah rarely took a step, or for that matter even stopped for a moment, with his feet on one branch that he did not support himself by a hand or tail holding an entirely different branch.

We stopped to sleep, rose to eat, finding fresh water trapped in occasional pools formed by the great tree limbs. Food there was aplenty—mostly small game and fruit. The going was slow among the thicker branches, but we moved steadily toward our destination, the head of the lake and marsh. Occasional glimpses through the trees of the water shining in the bright sunlight told us we had not yet reached our turning point.

Sometimes our progress disturbed flocks of birds or tiny flying reptiles. Little, brick-red pterodactyls, no bigger than my hand, flitted from tree to tree, hissing at us if we came too near. Sometimes there were breaks in the leaf cover and we could see the ground again—usually stretches of watery swamp or low trees. Here we would catch glimpses of the larger reptilian denizens of this strange world. Most of those we saw were the huge herbivores—the brontosaurus and its relatives, hordes of horned and neck-frilled triceratops and occasional armored stegosaurs. Usually all we could see would be a few grey-green backs and hear the crashing and sloshing of the big brutes in the undergrowth. There must be paths through the jungle for the monsters to find their way from one grazing ground to another.

Any thoughts I might have had of using the game trails ourselves was quickly dispelled by the sight of three or four horned and beaked triceratops crash-

178

ing through the trees after being startled by the attack of a predator lizard which looked like the giant tyrannosaurus we had seen previously—except that it was considerably smaller, standing a mere eight or ten feet above the ground when it was erect.

No, we were safer in the tree-tops, no matter what the dangers, and the dangers seemed, in perspective, to be slight. To be sure, I had nearly fallen to my death, but since then I had learned to climb with greater caution. Elkar had been stung by a wasp, and we all bore a variety of scrapes and scratches, but otherwise we had been perfectly safe. Our next biggest problem, as a matter of fact, turned out to be human rather than saurian.

We had "camped" on a series of broad branches. I had the first watch and I had been writing notes to Zed who perched on a branch near my head. The lack of paper and pencil was frustrating to both of us. I was trying to explain that the teeming reptile life around us was all extinct in the world of the outer crust. Zed frankly found this unbelievable.

"Are furred creatures so large and powerful that they can destroy the big killer lizards?" he wrote me on a series of broad leaves, using his claw for a stylus.

"No," I wrote back, "no beast of the outer world could really challenge them for size and ferocity." An outbreak of snarls and crashing noises from somewhere in the jungle to our left seemed to emphasize my statement. "We think changes in the climate or some new disease killed them all off, enabling the small furry ones to take over."

"Perhaps," wrote Zed. "Here there are warm and cold areas, and, of course, storms. But with the sun always in the center of the universe, no major change in climate can occur. In your world, exposed to the great airless spaces you tell me are between

179

the surface and your sun, I can easily understand changes occurring. It is a wonder to me your whole world does not freeze."

"Sometimes it has," I replied. "In the past, much of the land has been covered with the hard water that freezes." I did not know a Mahar word for ice.

"I am awake, Red Axe," Gash growled. "How much longer are you going to go on plotting with the Mahar? Does he offer safety for you and your mate if you betray the rest of us into captivity again?"

"The trouble with you, Gash," I said, as calmly as I could, "is that your own mind is so rotten that you expect only the worst of everyone else."

"You are a fool to trust the Mahar. He is probably leading us into a trap."

"I do not think so. You, I know, would do so if you could, but he, being a Mahar and a reptile, is probably more trustworthy than a Had-bar." How I was to remember those angry words later, and regret having said them!

Zed took off into the sun-drenched sky and I lay down next to Varna to sleep. Gash was still grumbling. The treetops swayed and creaked in the breeze, the insects hummed and the distant dinosaurs hooted and bellowed faintly. I fell instantly asleep.

I was awakened, hours later, by hoarse shouts and cries of triumph. I leaped to my feet, sure that we were being attacked by some new monster. The sight that met my eyes was even more terrifying than a tree-gryf or a thipdar. Mooh-lah and Elkar were struggling with two giant Sagoths! A third ape-man was advancing toward me, stone axe in his hand. The faithless Gash was nowhere to be seen.

I came up to my feet with a wooden spear in

my grip. There was no time to throw, my opponent was almost upon me. I leveled the hardwood point and lunged at him. The sharpened wood caught on his ribs and the spear shaft bent. It was the branch of a giant iron-wood we had passed miles back on our trek and the tip was sharpened only by a few blows of my axe. The ape-man snarled and seized the spear with his free hand. I threw my whole weight on him. The skin and ribs gave way and the wooden shaft tore through his chest and lung. He cried out and fell back, was caught and held by the thick mass of flowering vines behind him. I did not try to retrieve the spear, but left it sticking into him and drew my axe from its thong loop at my side.

The other two Sagoths were in trouble. We were lucky that this was only a scouting party and we were evenly matched. Despite their size and agility in the trees, the ape-men had met their match in the three desperate gilaks who now faced them. One of the hairy brutes was struggling with Mooh-lah who was choking him with his tail wrapped around the Sagoth's neck. The other had seized Elak, straining him back against a giant branch, attempting to get close enough to use his ferocious fangs or to hurl the man off the tree.

In an instant, I was at my friend's side, my steel bladed axe hissing in the air. Chop! The Sagoth was down in a pool of blood. Elkar and I turned to help our companion, but the third Sagoth had already had enough. He pulled the choking tail from his throat with both hands and hurled Mooh-lah from the tree limb on which they fought. The monkey-man hurtled into space between the boughs, but before he had fallen ten feet he caught himself with hands and feet and prehensile tail among the vines which hung from every branch. The Sagoth turned and fled, bounding along the swaying, shaking tree road until he was out of sight.

"Gah!" said Mooh-lah, shaking himself as he rejoined us, "again we are in debt to you for lives, Red Axe! But where is that worthless Gash? He was on guard. I think I will drop him from the highest tree into the mud of the nearest big lizard wallow."

"Indeed, where is he?" I echoed, and then, terrified, "and where is Varna?"

We looked about us in dismay. The two downed Sagoths lay behind us. Of Gash and the girl there was no sign.

"Where could they have gone?" I cried, the dreadful suspicion already dawning on my mind. "Did the Sagoths carry them off?"

"We saw only the three of those," replied Elkar. "We woke to the shaking of the tree as they rushed upon us. No warning did we get from the ugly one. In truth, I think he has deserted us—perhaps when he saw the Sagoths attack. He is not brave, that one."

"Agreed," I said, "it is just the sort of thing I would expect of the cowardly Had-bar. Besides, though I hate to admit it, he had reason to be angry with me anyway."

We investigated. My companions put the wounded Sagoth out of his misery and pitched the two bodies off the tree to fall crashing into the lower depths. Mooh-lah inspected the leafy pallet where Varna had been sleeping, and quickly found her stone knife among the leaves.

"I think the Had-bar has stolen her, Red Axe."

"I am certain of it," I agreed, desperate. "What can I do? Can you follow his trail?"

He eyed me quizzically. "Are you sure she did

not go with him willingly? In my country, if such is the case, the mate of the missing woman may not pursue or kill the abductor."

I was shocked and outraged. For a moment I fingered my axe and glared at my companion. How dare he question me in this way?

"I only ask, Red Axe," said Mooh-lah, seeing my expression. "You must think of this. It will take much time to track them . . ."

"And the Sagoths will soon be upon us all," reminded Elkar. "One has escaped, it will not take him long to gather a party to come after us."

"You are both right," I said, "I am sorry, Mooh-lah. I am sure my mate went unwillingly. If she was with one of you two I would not be sure, but she hates the Had-bar and he has long desired her. Elkar, too, is right—we must hurry, no matter what we do."

The tailed man grunted his acceptance of my apology. He crawled over the branches on his hands and knees inspecting moss, bark, vines and leaves.

"They seem to have moved into the jungle in the direction we were going, anyway," he said, finally. "That also takes them away from the direction in which the Sagoths came, so it seems. . . ." He broke off as there was a flapping of wings above us. Zed descended to a perch beside us and turned one eye toward me.

"Red Axe," said Elkar quickly, "you think you are the only one who can talk to the Mahar. Can we trust him? Perhaps he has brought the Sagoths down upon us."

I was wild with apprehension for Varna, captive now in the hands of Gash or the Sagoths. It was with difficulty that I kept my voice calm.

"I feel I can trust him. The rest of you must take

my word for it. There is no way I can convince you. He has helped us once, and for that, he tells me, his own people will kill him if they catch him."

On several sheets of tree bark I scrawled a note to Zed: "Disaster. Sagoths attack. We kill two, one escapes. My mate stolen by the other gilak or maybe other Sagoths."

The great pterodactyl read the message with a quick eye, made a gesture "Wait" in the air with a claw and flapped off, circling up over the tree tops above our heads. He disappeared. Mooh-lah continued his careful tracking.

"I will go ahead, looking for signs," he said, then I explained our situation. "The Had-bar must have taken her himself, there is no Sagoth smell anywhere here. You wait, see what the flying one says."

So, mad though I was to act, I had to literally sit and wait. Elkar collected a little fruit which he offered to share with me, but I impatiently gestured him aside. It seemed hours before Zed returned. Mooh-lah had gone off into the greenery. Of course, I had no way of knowing how long my wait had been, the sun remained directly overhead.

I had gathered some flat leaves for Zed to write on and I handed him a sheaf of these. Standing on the branch beside me, his wings folded so the fingers protruded up over his head, he balanced on one foot and wrote with the claws of the other, one or two Mahar characters on each leaf.

"Sagoths," he wrote, pointing back down the coast of the swamp, "Far away. See me. Searching for us. This way," he pointed forward, toward the jungle where Mooh-lah had gone. "Trees thin soon. More open. No gilaks seen. Sorry."

I gathered up the leaves and gave him a brief written message. "We go. Do you meet us where the trees thin out? Watch for my mate and her abductor."

Elkar and I set out along tangled branches that tied the towering trees together. Without our guide we moved slowly. Soon the green gloom swallowed us up. Mooh-lah had broken an occasional branch as he passed, and these kept us going. It seemed an eternity before the tailed man dropped from nowhere to a perch beside us.

"The Had-bar has been this way, I am sure," he said in reply to my anxious query. "Your mate is probably with him—I am not sure. Her scent is less strong than his, anyway, but I think I detect it—or some other female—occasionally. Perhaps he carries her."

"Good," said Elkar, "it will make him go more slowly."

I told Mooh-lah what Zed reported about the country to our front. He was pleased.

"It will make the ugly one easier to see if the trees thin out," he said. "Let us hurry."

I was in complete agreement. But when we began to see broad stretches between the trees, I was not encouraged. The ground was soft and boggy, much of it covered with tall reeds and tree ferns. Gash could be hiding anywhere in that undergrowth.

"Trail," said Mooh-lah, pointing. Trail indeed it was, winding off among the ferns, narrow, deserted —No! Now I could see two figures running towards us on that trail, running hard. In a moment, they reached the first of the big trees and the first figure —obviously a man—began to climb. When the second figure reached the tree and tried to climb, it was a woman, probably Varna, although still too far away to be sure. She was having trouble with her hands, but struggled to get a grip on a lower branch.

"Something must pursue them," grunted Mooh-lah.

Indeed, a moment later, a great carnivorous dinosaur broke into view. He was not jumping but stalking along on his huge, powerful hind legs, turning his head from side to side. The great green-grey head and its fanged mouth poised fifteen feet above ground.

At just that instant, the man in the tree—it had to be Gash—reached down and pulled the woman up into the tree. The killer saurian, however, caught sight of the movement and started, snarling, in that direction.

"It's Varna, I'm sure of it," I cried, "trapped by a tyrannosaurus!"

XIII

THE JAWS OF DEATH

The tyrannosaurus came crashing down the jungle path, crushing the heavy tree ferns and smaller trees under its taloned feet and lashing tail. It paused and turned its huge head, fanged mouth agape. The small fierce eyes scanned the lush greenery, searching for its prey. It sniffed the air, quiet, for a moment, then some movement of the two in the tree caught its eye. With a triumphant bellow, it rushed the tree, the great reptilian muzzle thrust among the branches, grasping the foliage with its puny forelimbs. The tree shook. The monster roared, the great jaws gnashed. It was too far to see clearly what was happening. We crouched on our tree limb, a hundred yards away, and prayed. The beast continued thrashing about, shaking the tree and growling like a pride of aroused lions. Then it became obvious that the great killer lizard was circling around to the other side of the tree. Could I see struggling human figures on the second tier of branches? The tyrannosaurus circled completely around the tree—fortunately it was a sturdy giant with a fifteen or twenty-foot diameter, and reappeared, renewing its attack on the branches on our side of the trunk. The vines and smaller branches were torn off and the snarling monster attacked the bark of the trunk, ripping it off in great sheets with its ineffective-looking forepaws.

"Uh, Red Axe," grunted Mooh-lah, grasping my shoulder with his strong right hand. He pointed at the upper reaches of the besieged tree, some fifty feet above the dinosaur's head. Yes, there were two figures crouched on a branch, gazing down on their pursuer! Even at this distance, I could make out Varna's black hair and naked feminine figure. Thank God she was still alive! Alive and undaunted, for she was obviously shouting taunts or imprecations on the great beast beneath. The tyrannosaurus was roaring and snarling and I could not hear her voice, but I could see her shout at the monster and throw leaves and twigs at it with her slender hand. Gash crouched at her side, gazing down fascinated. Neither of them had yet seen us in our tree.

"Mooh-lah," I said, "how do we get into that tree?"

He grunted again. "Not this way," he said, gesturing at the trees before us. "No tree close here. We seek the other side." Suiting action to words, he swung off around the clearing leaping from branch to branch with an agility that left Elkar and I panting in his wake.

When we caught up with our tailed friend, he was sitting on a limb as broad as a sidewalk, gazing out across the tops of the palms and ferns at the forest giant where the great carnivorous dinosaur still roared and tore up the ground with its talons. We had circled the besieged tree without finding an avenue to approach it.

Actually, the big tree did have branches touching its neighbors, but they were the fine, thin branches at the top and even Mooh-lah did not think it practical to cross with them.

"It is a tree we would have gone around," said Elkar, climbing up on the branch beside me and catching his breath.

"Yea, if it did not have such interesting fruit," I replied.

"It would be easy if there were not others interested in that fruit," rejoined Mooh-lah, pointing toward the tyrannosaurus, which had now taken up a position half squatting on its tail under the tree, its head thrown back to catch a glimpse of its prey.

"Yes, if it wasn't for him we could climb down and walk over," I agreed.

"Gash and the girl are not going anywhere," said Elkar. "We watch and wait. The big dryath will go away if we wait long enough."

Well, that was good advice, but I was in no mood to follow it. My mate was in that tree, and if the threat of the monster on the ground was not enough to drive me to her side, she was the captive of another man. I felt the situation called for desperate measures, and desperate indeed were the measures I adopted.

"Mooh-lah," I asked, "can we throw or swing a rope of vines to the other tree?"

The monkey-man squinted his eyes at the space between the isolated tree and our present arboreal perch. The tyrannosaur circled its base once more, snarling up into the foliage. We could see no sign of Gash or Varna.

"If I get my hands on that Had-bar," I muttered, "I'll break his neck!"

Mooh-lah grunted. "Too far to throw, Red Axe," he said, "maybe swing from upper branches to get enough distance. Can not be sure."

"Let's try it," I said, my teeth set. My companions looked at my face and shrugged. They knew better than to argue. Elkar remained on the branch we now occupied, about fifty feet above the ground, to keep watch. The tailed man and I went back to the tree trunk and ascended laboriously through a mass of leaves and vines and clinging plants to another branch hundreds of feet above. More dense masses of vines already hung down into the space beneath. Mooh-lah began selecting among them, weaving the longest and strongest tendrils together. I cut new lengths with my axe and these too he incorporated into his living green rope. It was hot tedious work in the full light of the Pellucidarian sun, but the occasional roars of the ferocious dinosaur below us kept us working. When we finished, we had a hauser of vines over two hundred feet long descending from our branch to hang below the level where Elkar stood beneath us.

Mooh-lah inspected his creation with a modicom of satisfaction. "Probably hold you a short while, Red Axe," he predicted. "We go back down now, start to swing you from below."

We climbed back down the trunk of the forest

giant, disturbing several green and yellow lizards as we did so. One of them spread tiny membranous wings and sailed off. "Too bad you can not do that," said Mooh-lah. It reminded me of the other member of our party—the one who could fly—but anxious scanning of the sky gave no glimpse of Zed.

I got my weapons securely tied to my body, knife at each hip, steel-bladed axe fastened on my back. I would need both hands to grab the foliage of the opposite tree when I got close to it. If I got to that point, I would probably wish for Mooh-lah's tail, also.

I braced myself on the vine rope, getting a secure purchase with both feet. "Shove off," I said to my comrades. They pulled me as far back as possible and push me over the brink. The first swing barely got me started, but each time I went by their limb, they gave me another shove and soon my trailing rope of greenery and I were sweeping out in wider and wider arcs. Fortunately, I have done a little sky diving and the swaying and the heights did not disturb me. What did, however, was the distance I had to cover. Mooh-lah and Elkar had braced themselves on the branch, one on either side of the point where my swinging path crossed their tree limb. They clung to the huge branch, their feet (and Mooh-lah's tail) grasping the mass of vines that encircled it. Each time I swept by they grasped the vine rope, or my body, whichever was closer, and pushed to increase the arc of my swing. Wilder and wilder grew the gyrations of the vines, and it was more difficult for them to catch me just right with a push. I found I could shift my weight up and down by crouching and then straightening my body and this would increase the force of the swing. Nearer and nearer came the distant tree. The vine rope creaked and stretched as if it was about to fall apart at any minute. I tried to pick out a branch to leap to if I got close enough, but the entire side of the tree before me was unbroken foliage.

Suddenly to my amazement, there was a face in the middle of it. There was a moment at the extreme extension of each swing when I seemed to hover motionless in the air. This was the ideal moment to scan my goal. At one of these moments, then, a round ugly brown head appeared among the leaves a little above and ahead of me.

"Eee-yah!" yelled the excited Had-bar, "Red Axel!" Then I was gone on the long sweep of my swing. I was still more than ten feet from the tree. Too far to jump. Also, I was reaching the maximum radius of my vine rope—it was almost horizontal at the end of each swing now. Back I came, throwing my weight against the creaking, twisting vines, hoping I could reach the tree at the end of the swing. The faces of my two friends were just a blur as I swished by, going at my maximum velocity. As I sailed out over the open space between the two trees, I glanced down to find the tyrannosaurus had circled around to this side of the tree and was gazing up at me as I swung back and forth. He was a good hundred feet below me, however, and I could care less what he thought. Gash was another matter. The ugly cave-man was just in front of me. I had to attack him quickly before he found a way to club or spear me as I swung past his perch. Up rushed the tree, and I thought I could see my enemy's ugly head still sticking out of the leaves gaping at me.

Was that Varna's face beside him? I had no time to tell. The rope began to pull apart and I was flung outward toward the tree. It was now or never. At the height of the swing, I leaped, both arms out, and clutched an armful of greenery to me as if my life depended upon it, as indeed it did. I heard a scream. The tyrannosaurus let out a bellow of rage—perhaps he had been confidently expecting me to fall into his jaws, I thought, scrambling to get a better grip on the tree branch before me. With that the branch snapped and I fell a short ten feet hung up in a mass of vines and then began a slower but unescapable fall through the rotten branches, vine tendrils, masses of orchids, old birds' nests, and thick ferns between myself and the ground. Varna screamed again. Somebody else yelled—I think it was me.

Fortunately, I wasn't knocked unconscious. If I had been, I would have never survived, for as I fell crashing down the side of the tree, I burst at last through a mass of leaves and plummeted a last three feet to land directly on the head of the startled tyrannosaurus!

I suppose it was a toss-up which of us was the most surprised. Then I heard those steel jaws close with a snap. He lowered his head to get at me with the little forepaws. I was ahead of him, though, and I slid down his neck and on down his back as if it was a bannister. It was the roughest, bumpiest bannister I ever tried to ride, however, for the beast's skin was covered with ragged scales and irregular knobs.

I could see the great tail lashing in the undergrowth and I had enough of my wits about me to know I wanted to avoid that flailing tail if I could. I checked my slide at the beast's hips and jumped six feet to the ground. The great saurian turned, snarling, to get me. Fortunately, he turned to the right, I had jumped down on his left. Before the monster had made a full turn to get at me, I had run among the roots of the trees and out of sight. The tree was a giant and huge buttresses of roots rose six feet on either side. Among these I scrambled, hearing the harsh breathing of the dinosaur as he hunted for me.

My only chance was to ascend the tree rapidly —before the tyrannosaurus could discover, reach me, and crunch me between those gigantic jaws. I dared not even pause to catch my breath. The monster was a good twenty feet tall—I had to get that high *before* he spotted me. I chose my climbing site —lots of vines and some broken tree ferns leaning against the trunk, and began my ascent. I had gotten to the first branch when a tremendous roar shook my grip on the vines. Looking down I found myself gazing into the wide open maw of the gigantic meat-eater. The teeth were nearly a foot long and shaped like a row of daggers. A number of them were broken off. The beast's tongue and palate were pinkish grey and his breath stank. In the depths of his throat I could see the dangling uvula jiggling up and down. Roar! went the huge mouth. Up! the tree went Red Axe the Magnificent getting the hell out of there as fast as he could.

Ten feet further I drew myself up on a broad branch and sat with the tyrannosaurus roaring below me. I had no intention of resting long, however. Somewhere in this tree was my darling Varna, and the villain Gash. They couldn't leave anymore than I could—not while the terrible reptilian engine of destruction continued to maintain his vigil below. And that worthy showed no sign of leaving us.

I was covered with scratches and bruises, and stained with leaf juice and vine sap, but I was unharmed. My weapons, even my meager loin cloth and rough leather belt and straps had all survived my ordeal. In a few moments I was rested and ready to start my search for the other two humans in the tree. As I turned to the trunk to resume my ascent, I heard above me the brief but unmistakable sound of a woman's scream. In retrospect it was not so much a sound of pain or fear, but more one of anger and surprise, but it sent me clambering upward in reckless haste.

So it was that I came crashing out through the branches onto a huge tree limb to behold my enemy Gash, crouched not a dozen feet away. He had his stone knife in his right hand, and his heavy-browed eyes were fixed on my face.

"Hold, Red Axe!" he cried, "if you come a step closer I cut the rope."

For a moment I could not perceive what he was talking about. I was looking for Varna. She had made no sound after that single cry, and she was nowhere in sight.

"You fool!" I yelled at the cave man, "You ugly Neanderthal ape, what have you done with her?"

From below me there came a cry. Varna's voice! Keeping a hand on the loops of vine encircling the tree trunk, I leaned out to look down. She hung a few feet below the branch, loops and loops of vine encircling her young body, binding her arms to her sides. She turned slowly back and forth like a cocooned victim of some monstrous spider, helpless. Below her, its huge bulk somewhat dwarfed by the height, the tyrannosaurus turned its fierce, hungry maw upward, watching us.

Gash's mocking eyes met mine. What a predicament! I was essentially unarmed, for although I still carried knives, and the steel axe, all were carefully strapped to me so that they would not be lost in my hurtling journey to the tree.

"Back," snarled Gash, "back and down, Red Axe, or your mate drops to the meat-eater below us."

I considered throwing myself at him—too risky, he might easily cut the vine rope under his hand

194

before I could get my hands on his throat. We might both go off the branch then, but that mattered little to me at the moment. I had flung myself across the jungle spaces, I had evaded the killer below solely to wreak my vengeance on this man. A red haze floated in my vision and foul murder held sway in my heart. Only a consideration of Varna's safety could have stopped me, but that was the threat the Had-bar now held in his knife hand.

"Go down the tree, Red Axe," he sneered. "Go down and lead the meat-eater away from here. When we have escaped, I may let your mate go. She is too evil-tempered for me, I no longer want her."

"No longer want her, you misbegotten son of a Sagoth, if you harm her, I'll cut you into little pieces and feed you to the wild dogs!"

He laughed. "Don't come near," he warned. "One step and I cut the rope."

"You'll not escape me, Gash," I said, stalling now for time. In the sky over the clearing appeared the flapping silhouette of a pterodactyl. Was it Zed? Or perhaps a thipdar hunting us all. "No matter how far you flee, I'll follow you to the end of Pellucidar."

"You talk big," shouted the squat, ugly cave man. "You think you can frighten Gash, the Had-bar? I'm not afraid of you! I could fight and kill you anytime."

"Come on then," I challenged. The tree limb was about three feet broad. I let go my hand on the vines behind me and took a step forward, holding up my hands. "I have no weapon now, Gash, come and kill me."

"Back, back!" he warned, "or I cut the rope!"

"You coward," I said. The flying reptile circled and came in towards us in a silent glide. I was sure it was Zed, but how was I to attract his attention or get his help? Perhaps I could distract Gash for just a moment. "Already my Mahar circles in for the kill." I said, pointing behind the Had-bar. He grinned again, his yellowed, worn teeth showing between bearded lips, his eyes never left my face.

"That's an old trick, Red Axe," he snarled. "You will never fool a warrior like me with that. Now turn around and start down the tree to the great dryath below us." He laughed, an ugly evil chuckle deep in his chest.

At that moment, however, two things happened that turned the tables on old Gash. One was that Zed spotted us from the air and came swooping down to land in the tree, checking his flight with a great flapping of his leathery wings. As Gash turned at the sound, I began my rush at him, hoping to catch him off guard and knock him from the tree. Immediately, there came a great crashing of tree limbs behind me and a loud shout in Mooh-lah's voice. I knew at once that the monkey-man had swung himself into the far side of the tree and was on his way to aid me. His timing, however, was disastrous, for Gash turned back and saw me, almost in mid air as I leaped for him. Slash! went his great stone knife into the loops of vine that supported Varna's body. Then I hit him, knocked him backward. He stumbled to his knees and fell across the limb. I thought I saw him drop the knife as he grasped the tree to keep from falling, but he had it attached to his wrist by a thong. In a moment he had regained his feet, for my blow had not been a hard one.

I had no time for him, however, for the loops of Varna's life line, some cut by that single knife stroke, some merely weakened, were giving away strand by strand!

I threw myself flat on the broad tree limb and reached around under it with my left hand, seized the rope that supported Varna and heaved upward. The weight almost drew me off the tree. My legs spread, I tried to wrap myself around the broad limb on which I sprawled. My right hand clawed the surface, clutched more loops of vine and stopped my fall. And there I hung, flat on my belly, unable to pull her up, afraid to let go, every muscle straining to support her weight and at the same time keep myself from slipping off the branch. Below us the tyrannosaurus bellowed, perhaps in anticipation.

I looked up. Gash was crawling towards me, on his hands and knees. He had regained his knife, and he now held it ready in his right hand. Again, that evil grin split his ugly face.

"Now, Red Axe," he gloated, "I am going to cut off the arm with which you cling so desperately and let you fall, and your ill-tempered mate with you."

I pulled up with all my might, but in that ungainly position I could not get the leverage to raise Varna with one hand. Gash crept closer. He was going cautiously for all his boastful talk. What stopped him, however, was his innate greed and my axe. The red-bladed axe was still strapped to my back, so Gash could hardly help noticing it as he approached me lying spread-eagled on my belly. The steel axe, which had saved my life so many times since I entered the inner world, did so once more, for Gash paused to cut it loose before casting me to the monster below. As he bent over me, I let go of the tree with my right hand and seized him around the legs. The cave man let out a cry of terror and struggled to hold his balance. My new grip on his legs—and braced as he was, he held—gave me a shift in my center of gravity and

I got my feet under me and pulled myself erect, still holding a death grip on Gash with my right arm, now around his chest, and still holding the vine rope, to which Varna was tied, firmly in my left hand.

Gash and I stood braced on the great tree branch, chest to chest, his head below mine, with my right arm encircling his body. His right hand, unfortunately, still held the knife and he drew it back to strike. I could not defend myself, for my left hand clung to the vine rope. But now I heard the thud of feet behind me and strong supple hands grasped my left wrist and the rope.

"Red Axe," said the voice of Mooh-lah, "I am behind you. I have the girl, let go of the vines, I will hold them."

Gash swung his knife arm up and back and shifted his grip on the handle for a downward stab. I let go of the rope of vines with a muttered prayer. As the Had-bar's stroke descended, my left hand came up to meet it, and the murderous cave man felt his wrist crushed in a grip more powerful than his own. Back and down I forced his arm, stepping forward, forcing him back so that Mooh-lah had room to maneuver the rope and its precious burden.

Gash twisted in my grip, trying to break away. He was whimpering now, for he had looked into my face and what he saw there made his skin turn cold. Sweat broke out over his face. I forced him back another step and bent him down with the power of my shoulders and back. We swayed to and fro on the tree limb a moment and then he gave a gasp as I shifted my grip, swung my right arm around his neck, and dropped to my knee, bringing my victim with me as I swung his right hand up behind his back until his fingers opened and he dropped his knife. Quickly I shifted, grabbed him by one thigh and stood up, holding him up and over my head. I raised him into the air and cast him out from the tree. He gave a piercing scream. The great brute below threw back his head and roared. The doomed cave man came hurtling through the branches as that terrible maw opened beneath him. The fierce white fangs flashed in the sunlight, the great red gullet yawned, the huge jaws snapped shut, and the scream was cut off. For a moment silence reigned in the jungle.

"Yo, Red Axe, well done," grunted Mooh-lah. "Now come and help me haul your she up to the tree. Too heavy for me to move alone."

A few moments later Varna lay safe in my arms, except for a few bruises and scrapes from being lowered over the side of the branch and then unceremoniously hauled back again, none the worse for the wear.

We all sat on the branch above the tyrannosaurus while he finished his grisly meal and then gazed hungrily up at us again. Varna laughed, holding on to me with both arms.

"He wanted me," she said, pointing downward, but meaning the Had-bar and not the dinosaur. "So he hit me over the head while I was sleeping and knocked me senseless. I know there are tribes that do that, but I think in most of them the men just threaten and the girl goes with them willingly. I'll bet even in the Had-bar tribe custom forbids stunning a girl while she's asleep!" Disgust was obvious in her tone.

"You don't have to tell me——" I began, but she interrupted angrily.

"Faugh, he never got near me! When I came to he tied my hands and lowered me to the ground since I could not climb with my hands tied. He was so afraid you would catch up with us that he kept me moving and didn't take time to rape me. Oh, he pushed me down on the trail a few times," she laughed, "but once I bit him on the ear and another time I kicked him in the groin, and then he contented himself with telling me what terrible things he was going to do to me when he got me home. "Tame me!" her voice was shrill with disbelief. "Tame me, a daughter of Val-an! Conceited brute!"

I was relaxed enough to laugh. The strain of the fight was gone and the blood-lust had drained out of me. I sat high in a tree with the best friends a man ever had, and we swung our heels and laughed together.

"No, Varna, no man will ever tame you," I agreed.

"Certainly not," she said, looking up at me. "You don't for a moment think you have tamed me, do you?"

"No, my darling, I don't think so, not for a moment."

XIV

OUT OF THE FRYING PAN. . . .

We sat there, Zed, Mooh-lah. Varna and I, with the great dinosaur prowling beneath us, until we were rested. I had thought we would have difficulty getting out of the tree, now that we were in it, but Mooh-lah was quick to reassure me.

"Never jump into a tree unless you can jump out, Red Axe," he said. "Come and see." We climbed up into the branches and found the place where he had landed. The monkey-man had made a far more skillful landing than I had, and tied to the branches was a slender vine, the length of which stretched out across the clearing to another forest giant.

Mooh-lah called and there came an answering voice, in a moment we saw Elkar among the distant branches. He waved. "Pull away!" he called. We reeled in the vine and soon had a stout rope of interwoven vines in our hands. After that it was simple to swing to safety, one at a time, using the thin vine to guide the swing back. I made the last trip over and Zed flew to a new perch nearby as I stepped off the rope to clasp the shoulder of Elkar.

"Good to see you still alive, Red Axe," he grinned. "Mooh-lah and I thought we had seen the last of you when you fell on top of the great meat-eater."

"I thought so myself," I admitted. We humans were full of good spirits and with good reason—we were rid of the sullen Gash and were all back together. Elkar had to hug Varna and hear the whole story of her abduction given over again. Zed, however, seemed jumpy. Finally, he flew away a few branches and returned with a strip of bark. I went to him and he laboriously traced the words, "Sagoth pursuit!" into the soft material with a claw.

"Where?" I asked aloud, and pointed vaguely in several directions. The great reptile indicated with one set of wing fingers. I called the others to us and explained.

"He would not be so persistent if they were not fairly close," I concluded.

"Ah," sighed Mooh-lah, "I had hoped for a rest. Very well then, off we go." He turned and trotted out along the branch, looking for good access to the adjoining trees.

I explained our decision to Zed by gestures and

thanked him for the attempt to aid me in my rescue for Varna. The creature looked at me thoughtfully with each eye, spread his bat-like wings and took off.

Being without wings, the rest of the party was reduced to scuttling along the tree limbs. The going was slower. We had entered a part of the jungle where the trees were farther apart. Many, like the one Varna and Gash had been treed in, were relatively isolated. Great shafts of sunlight entered through the forest roof and illuminated the ground. As a result, there was a lush carpet of palms and ferns below us. Through this we could see the huge head of the tyrannosaurus following us.

"That fellow has developed a taste for gilak meat," Elkar remarked, "and is waiting for us to throw him another meal."

"He'll wait a long while," I laughed. Looking down on the lumbering beast from a relatively safe perch fifty or a hundred feet above his head, he did not appear to be much of a menace. I would not have thought the hungry reptile's pursuit so amusing if I had known what trouble he was to give us later.

We moved along from tree to tree, sometimes swinging on the long jungle vines. Soon we had left the monster behind, although occasionally we could hear a bellow from somewhere in the greenery below us.

On we went, climbing, leaping, swinging from one giant tree to another. There were still plenty of tall trees, but now there were more low ones, almost of normal size. The forest was thinning out and we could catch glimpses of the swampy lake off to our left. Scores of birds and small pterodactyls were disturbed by our passage and rose in flocks about us. Once we passed around an open clearing where a little stream, a tributary to the lake, made a mud wallow. We had to leave our course for some distance, and as we came to the edge of the clearing, I scanned it anxiously wondering if we dared to descend to the ground and cross on foot.

"What do you think, Mooh-lah?" I asked. "It looks quiet."

The monkey-man sniffed the air speculatively. "The whole place smells of dryath," he reported. "Maybe still there. Can't tell."

At that moment, however, our doubts were dispelled by a gigantic coughing grunt from the swamp before us. A triple-horned head reared up out of the reeds and peered at us. It was the most incredible visage I had ever seen among the bizarre creatures of Pellucidar. The creature stood eight feet high at the shoulder and its face resembled a mask, an illusion heightened by the presence of a tall ruff or collar that folded up over its neck. Projecting forward over each tiny eye was a four foot long horn, while a shorter one grew rhinoceros-like from the nose. The mouth was a parrot beak and a great handful of swamp reeds dangled from it, half-chewed. The most incredible thing about the triceratops (for I recognized the beast from museum reconstructions) was its coloring. No museum would have dared to paint its animals the color that nature had lavished on this ugly brute. Its body was brownish green, but the great neck shield was yellow-green and rimmed with red while the rest of the face was deep purple. The bird-like beak was a bright scarlet and around each pig-like eye were concentric rings of white. The great horns were ivory, smooth and polished so that they gleamed in the bright noon-day sun.

"Hah!" gasped Elkar, beside me on the branch.

"I think we will not walk through that creature's meadow!"

"Agreed," I said. The monster turned his head this way and that, finally raising that rainbow-colored head to gaze into our tree. The beaked mouth opened again and he bellowed.

"He has sharp ears, that one," whispered Varna.

The triple-horned beast turned that incredible head again, still searching. Then we heard a snarling roar in the jungle behind us and we knew what the triceratops was anticipating. In a few minutes the huge form of the tyrannosaurus loomed between the trees. The spike-headed giant bellowed again and the great carnivore approached slowly, softly snarling, treading on his taloned rear legs as if he were on tiptoe. The triceratops did not yield but stood his ground, silent now except for a shuffling of his feet.

"Red Axe," whispered Mooh-lah, "a good time for us to be away. Let the three-horned one occupy the Had-bar-eater, perhaps that one will forget us and attack this larger prey."

"Perhaps," I replied, "but I think he makes a bad mistake if he does. Three-horns looks tough and mean. Unless I miss my guess, he's looking for a fight."

"Very well," agreed the tailed man, "but let us be gone when he has it. Follow me." With these words he seized a vine that hung from our tree and began lowering himself hand over hand to the ground. As I started down last, after Varna, I saw the triceratops lower its head, paw the ground like a bull and then rush the tyrannosaurus. The big man-eater was too quick to be caught off guard, however, and he dodged out of the way, snarling and clashing his jaws. When I reached the ground the dinosaurs were out of sight, although we could hear them moving about in the jungle close at hand. Hurriedly, we picked our way among the reeds and ferns of the marsh, Mooh-lah leading. The trees at the far side of the clearing suddenly looked very far away indeed. We were all armed with wooden spears, cut from the great tree branches with my axe, but they would be as useful as toothpicks against either of the great saurians if they attacked us.

The thick greenery gave way to more open grassy space as we neared the stream bed. Here we found the cause of the triceratop's pugnacious attitude, for in a bowl-like depression were a dozen huge eggs. Two of them had already hatched and the little triceratops, their horns not yet grown, big as pigs, were stumbling about awkwardly. They squealed in fright as we hurried by and it seemed that an answering bellow came from behind us. We lost no time in wading the shallow stream and running up the grassy slope on the other side.

The roars and crashing of vegetation behind us suggested pursuit, although perhaps it only meant that the two monsters had closed in combat with each other.

We did not wait to see. We were spread out in a ragged line now, Mooh-lah slightly in the lead, Varna between him and myself, Elkar bringing up the rear. We could see the edge of the tall jungle only a few hundred yards ahead. The big trees meant safety from the huge dinosaurs, if we could get up into them in time. Tired as I was, I was running easily now, when I saw Mooh-lah suddenly drop to his knees behind a clump of ferns and motion us to halt. Turning in my tracks I could see the huge silhouettes of the tyrannosaurus and his horned adversary against the backdrop of trees across the stream. They were close, but still preoccupied with each other. I crept forward to where Mooh-lah still crouched.

"What is it?"

"Sagoths," he hissed. "A group of them among the trees just ahead. I do not think they have seen us yet."

I peered cautiously through the ferns. A war party of at least twenty of the gorilla men was milling around just a hundred yards ahead of us. The leader carried a staff decorated with a human skull. He had halted his troop at the edge of the clearing, probably hearing the commotion the two dinosaurs were putting on. That did us no good, however, for there was no way we could reach the relative sanctuary of the trees without being seen.

"Too many to fight," I said. "We'll have to turn back."

A hideous outburst of snarls and screams broke out behind us.

"I think the big guys have finally got it together," I said. "Come on, now's as good a time as any."

But as we turned and started back down the flower studded slope to the stream there rose a shout behind us. Looking back, we could see that several of the leather-clad Sagoths had climbed into the trees, probably to see what all the noise was about. One of these had caught sight of us.

"Gilaks!" he shouted, swinging out from his perch and pointing with one hand as he clung to the vine-covered trunk with the other. "Gilaks!"

"Oh, hell," I cried, "come on, we'll angle away from the lizard fight," and I started running back the way we had come, unslinging my axe as I ran.

We had just reached the stream when luck turned against us again. Roaring and shrieking, the huge tyrannosaurus came leaping down the bank into the water. He turned his huge head back the way he had come, fanged mouth agape, he snarled defiance. Close behind came the lumbering triceratops. Intent on driving the predator away from its nest it charged in like a living tank. Crash! The great bodies came together. The tyrannosaurus clung for a moment to that spikey head, but the armored dinosaur kept right on boring in. The predator was forced to give ground, he leaped backward and was among us before we realized what had happened. A random swipe of the enormous tail sent Elkar sailing headlong into a fern brake. Varna and I flung ourselves to the ground as one taloned foot passed over us. The horned dinosaur paused at the edge of the stream and bellowed defiance. Step by step the great meat-eater backed away from his adversary. Great bleeding gashes in its belly attested to the fighting prowess of the aroused triceratops.

Varna and I lay motionless, our hands clutched together, hardly daring to breathe. The tyrannosaurus continued backing up—in a few moments he would be far enough away that we could try a run for it. Perhaps he would back into the army of Sagoths on the other side of the clearing. That was a vain hope, I realized, the big ape-men were clever enough not to tangle with the tyrant lizard.

The triceratops seemed inclined to follow up its advantage. Sniffing and snorting it plunged across the stream and up the slope after its retreating enemy. Varna and I rolled frantically out of its way as huge elephantine feet smashed the undergrowth near where we lay. The beast passed us and I kept rolling, not wanting to be hit by a swing of the mighty tail. The splash of cold water halted me as we rolled, arms still around each other, into the stream.

"Come on," I gasped, scrambling to my feet, "which way did the others go?"

"I don't know," Varna whispered, pushing her tangled hair out of her eyes, "but let's get back to the trees before one of those things comes after us."

We were close to the nest of the triceratops as we ran, so I took Varna's hand again and we hurried quickly past it and down stream about fifty yards before turning back to the trees. The screams and snarls of the tyrannosaurus sounded farther off and we slowed to a trot.

"I wish I knew where the others were," I grunted, "we'll have the devil's own time finding them with the Sagoths crawling all over the landscape."

We were running easily now with Varna in front of me. I had my axe in my right hand. We had lost our spears in the wild scramble to escape being trampled by the dinosaurs.

"Water ahead," gasped Varna. We pulled up for a moment. The great gray lake spread out before us. Beyond the landscape tipped up again, green with forest and lush mountains until it faded into the blue. Over the water circled long-beaked pterodactyls, bobbing and weaving, occasionally darting down to snatch at a fish unwary enough to rise close to the surface. The grassy, flowered slope descended to the water's edge, festooned with vines and flowering growth. The nearest trees were a mere fifty yards away, but as we turned towards them I saw an unmistakable ape-like form drop from the lower branches to the ground and vanish from sight.

"Wait, Varna!" I pulled back on her hand. She sank to the ground while I crouched beside her. "I think I saw something!" As I watched, another and another figure dropped from the trees in front of us.

"Sagoths! We're surrounded," I said. "Varna, can we get back the way we came?"

She clutched at my shoulder, "Christopher, look." The great tyrannosaurus had appeared on the slope above us. Silent he stood for a moment, surveying the scene. He was suspicious of something. Had he seen us? Did he sense our presence or that of the Sagoths? Behind us I heard a few shouts from the ape-men. Either they had spotted us or they were warning members of their party of the tyrannosaurus. The big lizard lifted his mighty head, snarled, and came straight at us!

"Down Varna," I hissed, "maybe he won't see us."

"I can't, Christopher," she whispered, "the ground is hot to touch."

"Huh?" I muttered. The tyrant lizard was coming closer.

"The ground here," she muttered, "it's boiling. It's . . . it's. . . ." I glanced down. The earth was seething at my feet. For a moment I stood there, half bent, staring at that weird sight in the bright sunlight of primitive Pellucidar. The great tyrannosaurus snarled. He had sighted us now. All the rage and frustration of the fruitless battle with the horned dinosaur was in that snarl. On he came, his giant strides shaking the earth.

"Run, Varna!" I shouted, springing up. "Run down to the beach, quickly!"

"Christopher," she cried, clutching at my hand, "come on! You can't stop him!" The tyrannosaurus opened that incredible death-dealing maw and roared. I could see every foot-long white fang in his gums as he charged down upon us. In the distance I could hear the shouts of the Sagoths as they spotted us. Varna clawed at my hand in a paroxysm of anxiety. At my feet the earth boiled and disappeared. A hole, only a few inches across appeared in the ground in front of me. I backed away, keeping just in front of the great saurian. Like a juggernaut of death he rushed towards us. . . . Only a few more strides. To his ferocious snarl was added a new sound, a high pitched continuous scream.

The great dinosaur crossed the boiling mud hole. His hideous roar was cut off in mid-breath. A ghastly red line appeared in his huge muzzle. The gigantic body lurched on, the red line appeared on the reptile's chest and belly. Blood gushed from the wound, drenching the fern-covered slope. The titanic lizard, split into two complete halves, pouring gore and entrail from each half, fell smoking and bloody at my very feet. The ear-splitting scream of destroyed air came to a sudden halt. A vast and unbelievable silence fell over the grassy meadow. I remained on my feet, the huge carcass of the dinosaur before me, holding Varna's hand as she knelt beside me.

"Christopher, what is it?" she whispered. "What happened? Is some new terror going to attack?"

I could hear questioning shouts from the jungle as the Sagoths conferred with their lookouts up in the trees.

Out of the underbrush farther up the slope burst the form of Mooh-lah, the monkey man. In his arms he held the pale body of Elkar, apparently unconscious. When he saw us, the tailed man halted in amazement, staring at the body of the severed tyrannosaurus on the blood-drenched grass.

"Ho, Red Axe," he called when he had recovered his usual composure, "are you going to tell me you did that with one blow of your axe?"

I laughed. "No, my friend, but come and join us. Walk around the big meat-eater. I am expecting something unusual to happen." Then, with relief, I saw a stainless steel tube rise out of the ground. On top of it a series of lenses revolved. Silently they turned, sweeping the landscape. The telescope-like eyes paused a minute at the carcass of the great dinosaur and swung on around until they were leveled at me. The turning of the lens head stopped. There was a pause. My companions stared at this apparition from the earth in wonder. Then a voice came out of the apparatus. A matter-of-fact voice, questioning in English.

"West, for God's sake, is that you?"

I let out a great sigh of relief. "Yes, it's me, Doc."

"Your appearance has changed considerably," the metallic voice commented, "and what on earth is this creature?"

"The one on the ground? I believe that is a Tyrannosaurus Rex. Your disintegration beam arrived just in time to slice it in two as it was about to devour us."

"Good heavens." The mechanical device was silent a moment.

"Christopher, what is it?" whispered Varna.

"Is it alive?" Mooh-lah asked. "It seems to speak to you. Is it friend or enemy? We have quite enough enemies already. Ask it to politely go away."

"It's not really alive," I hastened to reassure my brave comrades, "but it carries the voice of my friends from a place far away on the outer world I have told you about."

"Magic!" hissed the monkey man. He carefully laid Elkar's still unconscious body on the grass. I was glad to see the albino's chest moving regularly —he was still alive. Mooh-lah advanced toward the steel periscope.

"Careful, Mooh-lah," I cautioned. "It has great destructive powers. It is the thing which just killed the big meat-eater."

"Chris," the machine said, interrupting us, "we have a million questions. We are all delighted to see you whole and hearty and we are dying to know more about your companions and Holmes is practically beside himself about the tyrannosaurus. We have you all pictured on the big TV screen now. How are you fixed at the moment? Are you safe or are there more of those monsters about?"

"Well," I said, drawing a deep breath, "I must admit my situation is a bit precarious. There are no more dinosaurs about, as far as I know, although there is an excellent possibility that some other representative of the Cretaceous will appear. At the moment, my friends and I are standing with our backs to a large body of water surrounded by ferocious armed savages intent on capturing or destroying us. They may have been temporarily scared off by your miraculous appearance, but they will be upon us before long. To put it mildly, we need all the help we can get."

There was a long pause while the matter transmitter people on the surface held a conference. Varna and I tended to Elkar who was gradually regaining consciousness. There was no sign yet of the Sagoths, but if they rushed us, we were in a bad way. Our total armamentarium now consisted of my axe and one stone knife. We pillowed Elkar against the carcass of the great slain tyrannosaurus and the other three of us sat down on the thigh of the beast facing the periscope. A soft breeze was blowing over the lakeside meadow. The triceratops must have gone back to its nest, for there was no sound from upstream. Behind us we could hear some distant squawking from the small pterodactyls fishing in the lake. There were some random noises in the trees near us on either side, but if the ape-men were there, and we knew they must be watching, they were silent, waiting.

"Chris," said Doc's voice from the metal device

sticking up out of the ground in front of us. "I have an idea. We can't send you a gun of any kind, because the explosives detonate when they recombine at the far end of the beam. You can detach the disintegrator, however. It unscrews at the top of the borer head and is on a short power cable—you can then aim it any direction and we can power it from here."

I got quickly to my feet and went to the apparatus. It was still warm to the touch. The ruby lens of the disintegrator was set flush with the top of the device, but by digging my fingernails into the hair-line fitting around it, I got it to turn one quarter of a revolution.

"Red Axe!" called Mooh-lah. "The Sagoths are moving in the trees. I can see them now on both sides of us!"

"I'm trying," I grunted. "Damn it, Doc, this thing is jammed. I've nothing but my fingers to work with and I can't loosen it."

"Christopher," Varna's voice was anxious. "Thipdars over the tree tops, coming this way!"

"Wait one," said Doc's voice from the machine, "I'll send you some tools. A small section of the shiny steel post slid outward and objects began to fall from it into the soft mud and trampled grass. A screwdriver, a crescent wrench, an assortment of nuts and bolts, three Allen wrenches and a small hammer.

"Doc, what the hell are you doing?" I cried, "Is the machine falling apart?"

"No, no," he assured me, "we're just sending you anything that might be useful on the nose of the borer. Wait, here's a good one, try this." A small lever tool with a suction cup on one end fell to the ground.

"Good," I said, picking it up, wiping it off as

best I could with my hands. "Now, don't turn on the disintegrator until I get it off." I could hear shouts as the Sagoths started towards us across the open. I did not bother looking up—I concentrated on loosening the destructive front end of the earth borer. Small bits of dirt had fallen down into the groove between two of the rotating flanges that held it in place. I had to blow gently to loosen the grit and then twist the suction wrench and blow again. Slowly, thread by thread, the device unscrewed. When it was projecting a quarter inch above the nose of the borer, I detached the suction cup and applied a crescent wrench. The work went more quickly, but the wrench kept slipping and had to be retightened. There was more shouting around me. Mooh-lah hurled a challenge and was answered by someone who could only have been a few feet away. At that moment the threads ended and the disintegrator was loose in my hands! I pulled it free. It was a short tube, about three feet long and six inches in diameter and extremely heavy. A coil of wire led from one end back into the metal borer.

I turned to face our enemies. A dozen huge Sagoths were drawn up a scant ten paces away. The leader, identified by a string of skulls around his neck, stepped forward, brandishing a giant stone axe. The rest of his troop hung back, wary and ready.

"Kagota," grunted the ape-man, in the language of the inner world, "Surrender, gilaks!"

"Now!" I cried, pointing the thing in my hands at his chest. There was a burst of sound, a screaming whistle that hurt the ears as the air split by the barely visible purplish beam of the disintegrator ray. The big Sagoth had time to look down stupidly at his chest. There was a round, momentarily bloodless hole clean through it. He crumpled.

"Now, now, again!" I yelled, sweeping the death ray back and forth like water from the nozzle of a fire hose. The beam cut across the massed Sagoths, arms, heads and parts of torsos disappeared beneath it. The beam swept the forest behind them cutting down fifty trees which fell crashing, pulling other immense tree tops with them in a tangle of vines.

"Thipdars!" cried Varna, "the thipdars are upon us!" The cries of wounded and dying Sagoths filled the air. I glanced up just as a huge winged reptile soared over our heads. There were three of the beasts, and they all had Sagoth riders astride their necks.

"Power off!" I yelled. The disintegrator ceased its scream. I swung the muzzle of my incredible weapon about. The second flying dinosaur was swooping upon us.

"Turn it on!" My aim was wild, but it didn't matter, for I could swing the beam like a titanic sword of death. The pterodactyl hit it as if it were an invisible wall and flew apart—wings, severed head, ape-like rider and parts of the body fell to earth around us. I swung the beam back towards the one that had passed. The creature was making a great slow mid-air turn to come back to the attack. My ray cut a swath through both wings and sliced off its tail. It fell into the waters of the lake, instantly alive with snapping jaws as the carnivorous denizens of the depths rushed to the unexpected feast.

The Sagoth rider of the third thipdar had sense enough to try to avoid the fate of the first two. He turned his aerial steed and took off over the treetops, great wings flopping. My disintegrator tore the topmost branches off the nearest trees. He must have been at the extreme range of the ray, but I managed to wing him. The bat-like creature fell

215

into the greenery, and I saw its rider leap from his perch on the neck into the branches and, probably, to safety.

"Turn it off, turn it off." I shouted to my collaborators hundreds of miles away through the earth. Again the weapon went dead in my hands. Chunk! A six foot spear quivered upright in the ground at my feet. A yell from Mooh-lah and El-kar.

A quick glance around me showed where the trouble was. Another group of Sagoths—twenty or thirty strong—had come up the beach behind us.

"Turn it on! Quick!" More spears in the air. A flick of the disintegrator beam dissolved them in mid-flight. I swung the ray down into the lake. The water boiled. The beam swung shoreward. The ground in front of the Sagoths sliced open, dirt and rocks sprayed up upon them. Another slash with the beam, the terrified ape-men went down like wheat before the reaper. Chunks of earth and fragments of men and weapons went flying. The survivors took to their heels. I swept the far side of the meadow for good measure, catching the last of the Sagoth band there as the underbrush dissolved before the ravening fire of the disintegrator. Finally, I called for the surface men to shut the weapon off.

I stood in a field of carnage probably unequalled in the history of Pellucidar. Bleeding fragments of dead Sagoths littered the torn landscape. Trees and grass were cut flat in all directions. The ground was sliced open on either side of the dead tyrannosaurus and the lake still boiled and steamed where the ray had raked it.

I threw one arm around Varna and climbed to the top of one half of the dinosaur to survey the scene of my victory.

"There," I said with a flourish, "I guess that will hold them for a while!" And now, at last, I have come to the end of my narrative. We set up camp on the battlefield and the earth probe provided us with fresh hot food and a thermos jug of coffee which my Pellucidarian allies did not like, although they adored the hamburgers and milkshakes sent us courtesy of the drive-in down the street from the laboratory.

I have dictated this story, we have rested and Elkar seems recovered from his concussion. Zed rejoined us, much amazed at the carnage we had created and even more fascinated by the earth-borer. I put him into communication with the surface people, but I had to act as interpreter. After we had eaten and slept seven times, I realized that the Mahar scientist and his human counterparts on the surface would be perfectly happy to keep me there, transcribing messages for them, until I died of old age. Of course, in Pellucidar, nobody dies of old age. In this land of terrible beasts and savage men, everyone eventually meets a violent end.

"Look, Doc," I told the steel shaft, "we've put in enough time on this project for now. The scavengers have cleaned the bones of the tyrannosaurus until they are glistening white. Mooh-lah and Varna have to get back to their people and Elkar and I are going to see them there. I'll be sorry to leave the disintegrator, of course, it's a great little equalizer in this country of monstrous carnivores, but we'll manage without it. Maybe Zed will camp here and write to you for a while."

"But, Christopher," the distant surface men objected, "we arranged this probe to rescue you. We're devising a way to have you set up the disintegrator so that we can transport you back to the surface."

I looked about me. Across the camp fire Varna

crouched, her magnificent black hair pulled back with an ornamented thong. She was cooking some fish Mooh-lah had speared in the lake. She glanced shyly at me and smiled. Behind her loomed the white rib cage of the tyrannosaurus. Zed perched there, laboriously writing in a paper notepad with a ballpoint pen. Behind them loomed the endless green of the prehistoric jungle, looming up as far as the eye could see. Overhead hung the perpetual noonday sun of Pellucidar.

"You're crazy, Doc," I said. "Leave all this?" I gestured with a sweep of my arm. The lenses of the earth borer turned about in its turret as the surface man scanned the scene. "No, sir," I continued, "not on your life. Things are just getting interesting here. Set up the matter transmitter if you like. We'll send you some fresh dinosaur bones, or a triceratops egg. Maybe Zed would like to make the trip, but not me."

Seeing me looking at her, Varna got up and came over to me. I put my arms around her, gazing down into her huge brown eyes.

"I am going back to the land of Val-an with the most beautiful girl in two worlds," I said, in Pellucidarian, so that she could understand me. The periscope turned in my direction and paused, taking in the scene. Doc waited a moment before replying.

"Perhaps I understand your decision," he said.

FRITZ LEIBER

Just $1.25 each

The Big Time

Green Millennium

Swords Against Death

Swords and Deviltry

Swords Against Wizardry

Swords in the Mist

The Swords of Lankhmar

You're All Alone

Available wherever paperbacks are sold or use this coupon.

EDGAR RICE BURROUGHS

$1.50 each

Beyond the Farthest Star.

Cave Girl

The Deputy-Sheriff of
Comanche County

Eternal Savage

I am a Barbarian

The Lad And The Lion

The Land of Hidden Men

The Lost Continent

The Mad King

Mahars of Pellucidar Holmes

Master of Adventure Lupoff

Monster Men

Moon Maid

The Moon Men

The Mucker

The Oakdale Affair

Outlaw of Torn

Return Of The Mucker

The Rider

Available wherever paperbacks are sold or use this coupon.

EDGAR RICE BURROUGHS

$1.50 each

THE CASPAK SERIES

The Land Time Forgot

The People Time Forgot

Out of Time's Abyss

VENUS SERIES

The Pirates of Venus

Lost on Venus

Carson of Venus

Escape on Venus

The Wizard of Venus

INNER WORLD NOVELS

At Earth's Core

Pellucidar

Tanar of Pellucidar

Tarzan of the Earth's Core

Back to the Stone Age

Land of Terror

Savage Pellucidar

Available wherever paperbacks are sold or use this coupon.

16 I